BOTS

EMERGENT BEHAVIOR

Nicole M. Taylor

EPIC
Press

Emergent Behavior
Bots: Book #1

Written by Nicole M. Taylor

Copyright © 2016 by Abdo Consulting Group, Inc.

Published by EPIC Press™
PO Box 398166
Minneapolis, MN 55439

Printed in the United States of America.

Cover design by Dorothy Toth
Images for cover art obtained from iStockPhoto.com
Edited by Jennifer Skogen

LIBRARY OF CONGRESS CATALOGING-IN-PUBLICATION DATA

Taylor, Nicole M.
Emergent behavior / Nicole M. Taylor.
p. cm. — (Bots ; #1)
ISBN 978-1-68076-001-9 (hardcover)
1. Robots—Fiction. 2. Robotics—Fiction. 3. Young adult fiction. I. Title.
[Fic]—dc23

2015932711

EPICPRESS.COM

"Emergent Behavior": *Def. Unanticipated behavior demonstrated by a system. The result of interconnectivity, i.e., "the whole is greater than the sum of its parts." Inherently unpredictable.*

ONE

THE GIRL IN THE NEWSPAPER

MILLON, CALIFORNIA. WINTER, 2034

Edmond didn't know when exactly he had encountered his first slave. Maybe it was the young guy bussing tables at El Sept Mares. Maybe it was one of the dour middle-aged women working at the nail salon next to his barber. It could have been on the Number 32 bus, at the library, in any restaurant, or field of verdant crops.

He did know exactly when he encountered the most recent one.

The girl in the photograph had her head turned down to the side, tripping along in those absurd high heels made to look like sneakers. She was wearing a short skirt and a man's flannel jacket.

Underneath and to her right on the page there was another picture of her: what looked like a high school picture. Her face was fuller in the second photo. She had an eyebrow piercing and a single thin brown braid hanging down alongside her round cheek. She was not smiling in either picture.

MISSING TEENAGER FOUND IN SEX RING HORROR! the headline screamed, yet she wasn't missing. At least not as far as Edmond was concerned. He had known exactly where she was for months. She used to come into the gas station when Edmond was working, which was pretty often. She bought Pall Mall cigarettes and energy drinks. Once in a while, she would change things up and buy a package of gummy worms or a lotto scratcher. That skirt and that man's flannel shirt, she wore them all the time. She always had a lot of makeup on. The newspaper said she was a fifteen-year-old from Ohio who had run away from her foster family. It must have been the makeup that made her look older because Edmond had never realized, had never known, what she really was.

She would smile at Edmond sometimes when he handed her change. She waved her hand—a little desultory wiggle—when she walked out the door. He'd seen her pretty regularly for about eight months, talked with her, looked into her thinning face . . .

And she was a slave.

They didn't call her that in the paper: *Endangered, missing*. She had hooked up with some guy who wound up turning her out. The newspaper made it sound like an accident, as though this boyfriend had just stumbled into pimping out his underage girlfriend by sheer happenstance. Edmond could read between the lines: the girl in the newspaper was a slave, like thousands if not millions of others.

He tore the girl's picture out of the paper. For a very long time, he kept it in his wallet.

——o——

It wasn't that Edmond was particularly sentimental. Far from it, in fact. When he was eight years old, he had stunned his mother after she sat him down to tell him that his father was leaving their family. He had not cried or raged or even asked why. He wrinkled up his forehead as though working out a complex math problem. "That makes sense," he said finally. In those days, it was the highest praise he could bestow upon an idea or action.

It did make sense, though it took Wynette West years to admit as much. Edmond's father was a well-intentioned drunk, a dreamer who loved his family deeply but could never quite hurdle his own profound selfishness. He was already only a sporadic part of their lives, breezing in and out of town.

Not that day, but years later, Wynette was even able to laugh with Edmond about it. "God," she said. "Everybody must have thought I had something going with the mailman." What she meant, of course, was that it seemed impossible that Edmond's laughing Peter Pan of a father spawned a child who was never a child, not really.

They didn't even look alike. Edmond's father was a short, densely muscled man with sandy hair and a nearly constant affable grin. Edmond by contrast was tall and thin. "A reedy little fuck," his father used to say, not without affection. Wynette said that Edmond took after her own father, with his dark curls and the nearsightedness that necessitated glasses in the fifth grade.

Edmond didn't miss his father after he had gone because his father had rarely met any of his needs. His mother kept him fed and clothed, made sure he had school supplies and a ride home after robotics club. She was as consistent as the phases of the moon and Edmond appreciated routine. His father was an unpredictable variable, throwing him into the mix of their household offered more upset than anything else.

When Edmond was six, his father purchased a

small pony, completely unbidden. He said it was for Edmond, but it was wild and Edmond was not permitted to ride it for safety reasons. They tethered it in a little makeshift paddock behind the doublewide trailer that Edmond and his mother shared.

That was the strongest emotional memory that Edmond associated with his father: the bone-deep sadness that he felt when he looked out the kitchen window and saw that stunted little half-horse out there amongst the tall grasses. Edmond came home one day and found it missing. He had no idea who had taken the pony away or where it might have gone. He did not ask, however. Instead, he took over the ramshackle little shelter his father had built over the course of three days (and two twenty-four packs of Natural Ice).

It became his first workshop and lasted until he was fifteen when an unseasonable windstorm finally collapsed a load-bearing support. By then, Wynette had the gas station and she was making enough to move them into a real house. She let Edmond have the whole attic to himself. That was where he was living the summer the girl showed up in the newspaper.

An attic in Millon, California was not where Edmond West expected to be at age nineteen. Truthfully, it was not what anyone else had expected either. Though he had never been a popular boy, his classmates recognized something in him, some fundamental difference that set him apart from everyone else in their tiny town.

Wynette had gotten pregnant instead of completing her own undergraduate degree and had spent seventeen years almost solely focused on the task of getting Edmond to college. She would have been happy if he'd attended a lesser UC school or even a community college. Even just one step further than she herself had gone. Edmond had surprised no one by getting accepted to a number of top institutions, eventually deciding on MIT.

The day she packed him off for college was the culmination of half her life's work.

Edmond's stint at MIT lasted for three-and-a-half semesters.

People often said of Edmond that he was a "good boy," an "obedient boy," but he didn't necessarily agree. It had always been easy for him to obey because he had no pressing reason to do otherwise. Was he *good* if it had simply never much benefited him to be *bad*? Similarly, there had never been call to disappoint his mother before he showed up at her door one night with everything that mattered to him packed into the same backpack he'd used all through high school.

There was nothing Wynette could do to change this outcome, so she said nothing. She didn't have to. If she were to lecture him, it would be nothing compared to the litany of recriminations that played constantly in Edmond's own head. If she were to punish him, it would pale in comparison to the prospect of living in Millon for all of the foreseeable future.

If one held out a string, with one end being Los Angeles and the other San Francisco, the middle place—the place where it sagged and almost hit the dirt—would be Millon. People didn't move there so much as they slid downwards from either of those two poles.

Edmond had never been one for socialization, even before, when he'd had a legitimate excuse to be in town. If he was perfectly honest with himself, he was hiding out a little bit. He had no desire to run into people he had known from high school at the grocery store or post office. So he asked his mother if he could cover night shifts at the gas station for her. During the day he holed up in his workshop.

He wasn't really working, though he knew that's what his mother assumed. She probably thought he was pausing to regroup having found that the whole of MIT was not sufficient to contain his brilliance.

In truth, Edmond was experiencing something he'd almost never encountered before: uncertainty.

Edmond didn't know exactly what he had been expecting from college, perhaps simply that elusive *more*. He expected to feel as though, after years of striving towards it, the useful part of his life had finally begun. Instead, he found a sea of awkward children: just brighter versions of the people he'd known and avoided in high school. He found himself to be all alone yet again.

He was sure that they would feel, like he did, that there was a great task set before them—a broken world that was theirs to reshape and repair. Yet there was no clarity of vision, not a plan of action amongst them. Oh, certainly many of them could say which companies they wanted to work for—or start—or generally what sort of work they would like to do. But as to their mark, the measurable change they would make in this world in their short lives? All Edmond ever got was a shrug, a blank look of confusion from all those bright young things used to grasping everything so easily. It nearly drove him mad.

———o———

Edmond followed news of the girl in the paper, but there was little more about her specifically. Instead there was a small series on what the paper was calling a "prostitution ring" run out of the local motel, The Circle Inn. Edmond had never known whether that name was supposed to be a pun or not.

It was the only motel in town or at least it had been until a year ago when the Motel 6 went up by the freeway. Edmond didn't know anyone who had ever actually stayed there, but all the kids in town knew it nonetheless. They charged two dollars at the desk for an afternoon's swim in the dingy little pool. Edmond had forked over his crumpled pocket change along with the rest of them.

He hadn't been there in years however. Most

of the kids stopped going right around the time they got their driver's licenses and, God, who would want to spend the night there? Edmond wasn't sure how the business stayed afloat. Probably lost and desperate travelers on their way to somewhere better.

Two weeks after the girl appeared in the newspaper, Edmond got off the night shift at six a.m. and found himself driving towards the edge of town to The Circle Inn. He pulled into the parking lot still a little bleary from a long night languishing behind the counter at the gas station. He rubbed his eyes and took a long, critical look at the motel.

There was no outward indication that anything untoward had happened there. No crime scene tape, no gaping-open doors, no official notices pasted up. It looked like business as usual insofar as the place had business. There was just one other car in the parking lot and a slumped figure behind the front desk.

When Edmond was young, Terry Pascal was a zit-faced teenager, working sullenly for his father. Now he apparently owned the place outright, though his feelings about the work seemed much the same. His hair was shorter and he had put on weight, but he was otherwise unchanged. He slouched behind the desk, looking vacantly at a bulky desktop computer monitor. A truly disgusting keyboard sat in front of him next to a half-eaten honeybun.

"Hey," Edmond said. Terry barely twitched. "Mmm?"

"Is this where the prostitution thing was?" Edmond knew perfectly well that it was but it seemed impossible that the place could be so unchanged by what had happened; that Terry himself could be so nonchalant.

"Yep," Terry answered. For the first time, he moved. He reached over and picked up the honeybun. He took a single bite and then set it back down.

"Which room?" Edmond asked.

Terry finally looked at him. "Huh?"

"Which room were they working out of?"

"Bunch of 'em," Terry said, between additional bites of honeybun. "Five or six, I guess."

That was disconcerting. The Circle Inn was a single-story building shaped—as the name might imply—like the letter C. Edmond doubted there were more than ten or twelve rooms total.

"Can I see it?" Edmond asked. Terry cocked his head at him like a confused dog wondering where the next treat was coming from.

"What?"

"The room. The room they used. One of them."

Terry looked down at his honeybun in consternation as though the pastry had some conclusion to offer him. "Unless you're a cop, you've gotta pay," he pronounced finally, seemingly pleased with his solution to the thorny problem Edmond had posed to him.

Edmond sighed and produced his wallet. His mother insisted on paying him a wage for his shifts at the gas station though he had little need for money at the moment. Perhaps it was his mother's subtle way of suggesting he get his own apartment.

The Circle Inn was still using actual metal keys. Edmond turned it over in his hands, a little surprised. "Room 4," Terry told him. "It's the fourth door."

"Thanks for the tip," Edmond said.

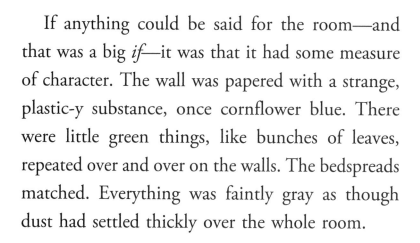

If anything could be said for the room—and that was a big *if*—it was that it had some measure of character. The wall was papered with a strange, plastic-y substance, once cornflower blue. There were little green things, like bunches of leaves, repeated over and over on the walls. The bedspreads matched. Everything was faintly gray as though dust had settled thickly over the whole room.

There were two twin beds and a single soft chair facing them. There was no TV, microwave, or mini-fridge. Not even an ice bucket. Someone had left a small pile of unwrapped bars of soap on the bedside table. Everything smelled like cigarettes.

Edmond sat down on the end of the bed. It didn't so much sag underneath him as tilt—the whole mattress moving as one. He closed his eyes and imagined this place being the first thing he saw in the morning, the last thing he saw before he slept.

The bedspread underneath him was neat and more or less unwrinkled. Simply looking around, Edmond might not have imagined that something horrible had happened here. At least no more horrible than the standard parade of poor decisions that occurred in such settings.

Four or five rooms just like this one. The ring had run out of half the motel. Clientele necessarily included a healthy proportion of locals as well as anonymous visitors. This was not an act of junkie desperation, it was organized and deliberate. It was an enterprise. It was a sophisticated one as well because it was the girl who was in the paper now, the girl who was being led back to her foster parents with her head hanging down like a celebrity sneaking out of a hotel. And the boyfriend who had brought her here? On that subject, the newspaper had nothing at all to offer.

Edmond reached over and picked up one of the little naked soaps.

Edmond had never visited these rooms as a child, but he knew that they would have looked just the same back then. Fifteen years and not one thing would have changed.

Edmond left then and got back in his car. He took the little metal key and tucked it in his pocket. He couldn't say exactly why he did it: only that he wanted to take something, either from Terry or from the motel or from the town itself. He had done something like it before during those increasingly monotonous days at MIT. He had surprised himself one day in the school store by slipping a small flashlight keychain into his pocket. He challenged himself to take larger and larger objects, eventually working himself up to big textbooks for classes he wasn't even taking, like Beginning Architecture and Agriculture. It felt like an act of aggression, a lashing out against a school that had fallen so short of his expectations. It felt absurdly like a protest.

Now slipping the heavy key and the leather fob into his pocket, it felt like the least he could do.

—o—

Edmond had asked his mother once why she had given him such an oddly formal name, a name that invariably stuck out amongst the Codys and Jaidens of his elementary school.

His mother, who had struggled under the weight of her own unusual name, just smiled at him. "It sounded like the name of an important man. And I knew you were going to be an important man." For the first nineteen years of his life, Edmond had believed her.

Since his return, Edmond had spent most of his free time looking through old, half-finished projects. There was a lot of junk there—things he was ashamed to admit he'd started just a year or two before. But there were some interesting things as well.

The most compelling by far was the functional animatronic hand he had been working on the winter before he left for college. It was made of a lightweight yet strong carbon alloy, a skeletal set of four fingers and a thumb, which he had programmed to perform certain basic functions. It could wave two different ways (finger-wiggle and wrist-turn), it could throw up a peace sign, and close itself tightly into a fist. It had been the prize of the robotics club: the fluidity of the movement and the exquisitely realistic interplay between the fingers and palm alone set it apart from anything anyone else was doing. Edmond had always been a little disappointed with the hand, but he was alone in that assessment.

The robotics club guys (and they were mostly guys, except for two intrepid girls named, coincidentally enough, Kelsey A. and Kelsey P.) effused over the thing. They suggested that he program it to manipulate objects, pick up delicate things, or even play an instrument. Truly, the possibilities were endless, but none of them had excited Edmond. Eventually he had abandoned the idea around the same time he withdrew from the robotics club. They had been salivating over the prospect of entering the hand in the yearly Central Coast Robotics Expo and they never really forgave Edmond for leaving the club and taking his work with him.

When he returned from The Circle Inn, he sat in his workshop and ran the hand through its limited repertoire again and again and again. It was a novelty, a joke. It had no value save to proclaim his own cleverness. So he could make a robotic hand that played the flute or picked up a playing card—what use was that?

The world was in need of hands. It needed hands to mine ore and harvest food and clean houses and cook and build laptops and shoes and everything under the sun. The demand was so great for useful hands, and here Edmond had contributed a single useless one and considered himself brilliant for having done so.

In theory, he thought he could redesign the hand. Allow it to do so much more than a prescribed set of motions. It could perform any function that a human hand could perform and it would do so without experiencing pain or weakness or fatigue.

Edmond tried to remember the newspaper girl's hands and found that he could not. Surely he had seen them as she pulled money from the inside pocket of her skirt. Maybe he had even touched them when she accepted her change. Had her fingers been long and delicate or short and stubbed? Did she paint her nails or accumulate dirt underneath them? Did she bite her nails perhaps? Wear a ring, a bracelet, freckles, scars?

She had not been picked for her hands, Edmond thought. His artificial one would not have saved her. So what was the point? She had been chosen for her simple, vulnerable humanity. It was still one of the cheapest commodities in the world and as of yet, there was no viable synthetic alternative. Edmond stuck on this thought for a while.

Beside him, the hand waved, a little desultory wiggle. Finally, Edmond stopped the machine, left those fingers frozen in mid-movement. Then he reached over and wrapped his own hand around the palm, and laced his fleshy digits through the metal ones. It was cold.

That was the first thing he would have to address.

TWO

THE ROBO EXPO

Fʀᴇꜱɴᴏ, Cᴀʟɪꜰᴏʀɴɪᴀ. Sᴘʀɪɴɢ 2035

Technically, Damsel had neither sex nor gender. A humanoid automaton that stopped abruptly at the waist, Edmond had not given her secondary—or primary—sex characteristics. Her chest was a single undifferentiated plate, smooth and metallic. He had labored over her face, but not in terms of aesthetics. After several failed trials, Edmond had discovered that there wasn't yet a synthetic material that mimicked human skin to his satisfaction.

So he had left her face bare.

Her eyes, partially functional little machines that he had designed himself, hovered, gelid and eerie, inside metal sockets. She had perfect, enameled teeth but no lips, a wired tangle where a nose might have gone. It seemed insane that anyone might have looked at her face and thought of a woman, yet Edmond did. Since the earliest days of her design, he had thought of her as a *she*.

Perhaps that was why when the time came to give her a name he called her Damsel.

Damsel's most critical function, as far as Edmond was concerned, was her ability to gesture. He had spent weeks refining her jointed limbs, her individual metal fingers, to make sure that they moved as easily and naturally as a real human's. The element that really set Damsel apart, though, was her capacity to learn. She could constantly add new gestures to her repertoire by watching others perform them.

Edmond had nearly reached the limit of what he felt he could teach her by himself alone in his attic—mimicking happiness, sadness, jubilation, rage. It was for that reason more than any of the others, that he was looking forward to the Central Coast Robotics Exposition. Damsel would have access to so many people who would move and gesture entirely unconscious of her. Edmond had never been much of an actor after all and it would be better for Damsel to see real physical expressions of emotions rather than his weak pantomimes.

In a way the Robo Expo would be Edmond's entrance—or re-entrance—into the world as well as Damsel's. He had more or less confined himself to his attic workshop in recent months working relentlessly on all of Damsel's individual components. After so long without a project to occupy him, it was satisfying to be at work again, even though it meant forgoing food and sleep to maximize a day's paltry twenty-four hours.

He still wasn't entirely sure that Damsel was ready to show to outsiders. She certainly wasn't everything he wanted her to be, but he also knew that realizing her fullest potential would take time and materials he didn't have. Possibly materials that didn't even exist. Nevertheless this was important. It was a test drive of sorts. Or a blind date.

His hands were sweating and he and his mom loaded Damsel into the backseat of his car. She was only three feet from skull to base, but she was fairly heavy. In the future, Edmond had plans to use lighter (and much more expensive) alloys for her skeleton.

"Ugh," his mother said, dropping Damsel down onto the leather seat. "That thing looks like something out of a nightmare," she said. Edmond had been living so closely with Damsel for so many months now he had nearly forgotten that this was also the first time his mother was seeing her.

"It's the nose," Edmond said. "Anything that doesn't have a nose is creepy." He reached across the metal woman to buckle her seatbelt.

Wynette shook her head at her ever-bewildering son. "Well, I hope you win."

"It's not really about winning," Edmond

informed her. "The real idea is to catch some investor's eye. Get some buzz going."

"Well, I hope you get buzzed then."

She insisted on hugging Edmond goodbye and she remained in the driveway, waving a little wave whenever he looked in the rearview window. She always seemed to know whenever his eyes flicked back towards her. As he drove, Edmond was very conscious of Damsel in the backseat. It was like driving with an old friend with whom he could comfortably remain silent.

—o—

The Expo was a demographic mish-mash. For every table staffed by earnest, pimpled high schoolers, there was a flashy station belonging to some startup tangentially related to robotics. All those guys were wearing polo shirts and constantly swiping at their flex-tablets. The attendees were similarly diverse: tech geeks comingled with bewildered parents and their eager young children.

Edmond was assigned a table close to an exit door, which made it mercifully easy to tote Damsel inside and set her up on the little card table provided. Edmond sincerely hoped the spindly legs would hold out under Damsel's weight.

Edmond fussed about her, making sure she had the best possible view of the passers-by before finally powering her on. Damsel came to life with a soft, dull buzz. Her teeth opened and then shut again. *Click.* Her eyes moved, roving over the people with hawkish attention to detail.

All at once, Edmond lost interest in the crowd. Now he was fixated on his brilliant machine. For the first time, he was getting to see her work from the outside looking in. It was mesmerizing. She scanned the room looking for appropriate targets for mimicry. Eventually her eyes alighted upon a middle-aged woman walking with her husband. The woman was speaking animatedly and she slapped the side of her hand into the palm of the other as though she were trying to cut through her own skin.

With a silken whisper of metal moving against itself, Damsel lifted her hands and mimicked the woman's actions exactly. She was performing exactly as intended and Edmond couldn't have been happier. Then she did something that Edmond hadn't anticipated: she turned her head to look at him. There was a sly cant to her face, as though she were asking for his approval or even showing off. Edmond had never seen her do anything like that before.

Uncertain how to react, Edmond found himself nodding at her as he would a child who had performed well. For some reason, it felt like the correct response. Damsel apparently accepted this because she turned her face back towards the crowd and ignored him again.

Damsel did not see the girl because she was well below her eye line. Edmond did not notice her because she was moving fast, weaving wildly between clumps of people. That was the very same reason in fact that the girl failed to notice the table leg—and ran directly into it.

The bony ridge of her eyebrow connected with the table's edge and she went down immediately.

"Whoa!" Edmond cried out, circling around the corner of the table to attend to her. It was probably bad form, but he could not help noticing that Damsel had reacted as well, with a quick jolt. Edmond had to admit that her jolting could have been a result of the table itself being jostled. Still, it was interesting. When Edmond went to help the girl, however, Damsel unmistakably leaned forward as far as she could manage. She stretched out both of her arms exactly as Edmond's own arms were outstretched towards the girl.

The girl was sobbing and the skin above her eye was already red and puffy. She was holding a quivering hand over her eye and Edmond couldn't tell if she'd done more damage than a simple bruise.

"Let me look," Edmond said severely. Startled, the girl dropped her hand and, for a moment at least, swallowed her tears. Her eye looked fine. Watery, but fine. She would probably have a shiner but Edmond doubted there would be any lasting damage.

"You're okay," he informed her in a slightly gentler tone.

"Yeah," the girl said softly, almost to herself. Edmond helped her to her feet and then looked around the room. There didn't appear to be any nervous parents flocking to the scene, despite the girl's hysterics.

"Where's your mother?"

"San Francisco," the girl answered. A factual answer, certainly, but also an unhelpful one. Edmond sighed.

"Who are you here with?"

"My dad." She had taken on that insufferable

tone that intelligent children had when they felt that an adult was being particularly obtuse.

"And where is he?"

"I don't know," she snapped. "I thought I saw him. I was running to catch up."

She was still holding her hand over her eye like a tiny cut-rate pirate. Edmond was bad at guessing children's ages, but he thought she was maybe eight or nine. Her long hair was in a neat braid and her clothes were clean and matched one another. She appeared to be a looked-after child. Her father was probably in the bathroom or engrossed in another exhibit.

Just as Edmond was wondering if there was a security station where he could deposit her, an authoritative voice called out: "Shannon!"

The girl perked up immediately.

A man, presumably Shannon's father, was striding down the central aisle. Unlike his daughter, he didn't dodge between people. Instead they seemed to part before him almost unconsciously as though his purposefulness was a force field that extended several feet in front of him.

He was a tall and unremarkable-looking man. His hair was black and thick and very neat. He was clean-shaven and dressed like a corporate cubicle dweller on his day off. He and his daughter had identical noses.

"What are you doing?" he asked. "Why are you holding your eye?"

Shannon gestured vaguely towards the table. "I hit my head."

"Were you running?" His tone suggested this was an old argument. Shannon said nothing, but she didn't look at him directly either. On the table, Damsel tilted her own face downwards. This small motion must have attracted Shannon's attention. Her eyes widened.

"Who's that?" the little girl asked.

"That's an automaton," her father answered before Edmond could get an explanation out.

Edmond bristled slightly. Automatons were

toys. Silly objects of curiosity for people in the nineteenth century. They could run through a set series of actions like serving tea, appearing to drink water, or writing a stock phrase. Damsel may not have been everything Edmond had hoped for, but she was far outside that class of machine.

Shannon, however, didn't seem to have registered her father's scorn. She stared avidly at Damsel. For a long moment, the metal woman and the girl observed one another with identical intensity. Then slowly Shannon reached her hand towards her own face and pretended to pick her nose. After a pause that somehow felt confused, Damsel did the same. Shannon erupted into laughter.

"It mirrors gestures." Her father sounded slightly more interested now. Damsel turned her head to look at him when spoke. The movement seemed to have surprised him because he looked at Edmond, scrutinizing him carefully for the first time.

"Hiram Liao," the man said, sticking out his hand. His handshake was very firm.

"Edmond West," Edmond answered.

Liao didn't exactly smile, but one side of his mouth quirked up slightly. "Do people ever just call you Ed?"

"Do people call you Hi?"

Liao snorted and turned his attention back to Damsel. "How many individual gestures can it reproduce?"

"Theoretically? An infinite number, I suppose. How many gestures can a human make?"

Shannon stood up on her tiptoes and tilted her face up towards Damsel, sticking out her pointed red tongue. Damsel had no tongue. She opened her teeth but there was nothing but a shallow void.

"Can't do that!" Shannon said triumphantly.

WHAM!

They all flinched as one. Damsel had balled her articulate hand into a fist and smashed it loudly onto the table's surface. The table itself wobbled with the force of the blow. Edmond wondered how sturdy the Expo's set up actually was.

"I'm sorry," Shannon said, sounding genuinely contrite. She was looking at Damsel and not at Edmond.

Liao gave his daughter a long look. "How do you get it to match gestures to the relevant emotions?"

Damsel lifted her head, looking out past all of them at the crowd. Her face upright and cold reminded Edmond of a gargoyle on a medieval church. A sentinel.

"I call her Damsel," Edmond said. "And I don't have any control over how she reacts in a given situation. She is a learning machine, I assume she is contextualizing these movements as she acquires more data about them."

"That would be impressive."

Edmond cocked his head. "*Would* be?"

"Well, I would want to observe the machine in closed laboratory conditions before I could properly evaluate its functions," Liao explained, as though Edmond had asked him to evaluate anything. The arrogance was astounding and Edmond was about to ask the man to collect his daughter and leave when Damsel moved, surprising him with her speed.

She reached out her arms like before and leaned down. Before Shannon could react, Damsel grabbed the girl around the waist and lifted her into the air. There was a charmed instant where no one moved or spoke or even seemed to breathe.

Edmond broke the spell first, he reached for Damsel's power supply just as Shannon started to squirm in the metal woman's grasp. To Edmond's great surprise, however, Liao reached over and grabbed his arm.

"Don't," he said. "Wait."

Shannon looked anxiously between her father and Damsel. She was roughly eye level with the machine now and Damsel's face was perhaps three inches from hers.

Liao still had his hand on Edmond's arm, but the man seemed totally calm, almost inert. Edmond by contrast was a single raw nerve. Because of the alloy that Edmond had used in her construction, Damsel had an extraordinary amount of power. She had a crush-strength of nearly three hundred pounds. Each hand was individually stronger than a pit bull's bite. And little Shannon Liao now rested uneasily between both of them.

"Damsel," Edmond said. Her name leaked out of him like a moan of pain.

And then Damsel moved. She lifted Shannon slightly and pulled her close. Finally she pressed her lipless mouth against the child's. Shannon's eyes darted back and forth wildly as she was held inexorably against the hard enamel of Damsel's teeth.

Damsel pulled away and returned the girl to the floor as gently as a mother cat depositing a kitten on the ground. Shannon sidled slowly over to her father, keeping her eyes on Damsel all the while. She leaned into Liao's leg and he patted the top of her head.

Liao smiled at him as though Damsel—or

perhaps Edmond—had passed some sort of test. "Where are you working right now?"

Edmond was stunned into honesty: "My mother's attic."

Liao reached into his pants pocket and produced a wallet. "If you'd like some better accommodations, give me a call." He withdrew a white business card from the wallet and handed it to Edmond. The script was both elegant and boilerplate. The words were slightly embossed and when Edmond moved the card the letters caught the light.

General Hiram Liao, it said. *United States Armed Forces.*

THREE

THE HOME OF THE BRAVE

SAN DOMENICA, CALIFORNIA. FALL 2035

General Liao's guided tour left a little something to be desired.

"The men's room is down there." Liao pointed vaguely at a hallway peeling off to the right.

"Storage." A closed door.

"There are some research pods in the connected building." A large set of metal exit doors.

"Kitchen facilities are upstairs." Liao didn't even bother to point in any particular direction for that one.

Edmond had actually been surprised to discover that Liao was undertaking this particular task himself. Didn't a General have better things to do than show newbies how to work the electric tea kettle? General Liao certainly acted like he had somewhere better to be.

The remoteness of the laboratory compound had surprised Edmond. During their initial meetings, Liao had described it only vaguely, saying that it was "in the South Bay." Edmond had been expecting some gleaming Silicon Valley tower or at least a funky campus with a lot of public art. Instead, it was far from anything approaching a real town—out in a blasted wilderness that reminded Edmond, quite honestly, of Millon.

A series of gray, boxy buildings were the only thing interrupting the scrubland. A mountain on one side formed a natural barrier to cars passing by on the nearby freeway and the interior of the compound was swaddled in a black, barb-wire fence. It looked like the most advanced piece of technology on the whole lot.

The road to get into the place was so narrow and poorly maintained that for several miles Edmond had assumed it was an old fire road. Nevertheless there were still signs plastered all over the route, warning motorists that they were trespassing on a military installation. TURN BACK NOW, one read in ten-inch capital letters.

Edmond assumed that it wasn't *just* a laboratory. Apparently, the lab portion occupied only one of the squat silvery boxes. When he asked about the other four, Liao had told him simply that those were "not relevant to his interests."

It was the kind of place, Edmond figured, where the Army might put an alien corpse or a secret nuclear bunker. Somehow, he had imagined starting work at such a place would be more exciting. So far, it had been all paperwork and the world's most unhelpful tour.

The current long hallway terminated in a metal door painted Army green, naturally. There was a small window, the glass crisscrossed with metal wires. Next to the handle there was a keypad and an understated black box that looked a little like a garage door opener.

General Liao pulled a plastic ID card from his breast pocket and waved it in front of the black box. After a dull beep, he quickly entered a number into the keypad. He didn't try to hide the keypad from Edmond and, although Liao's fingers moved rapidly, Edmond couldn't help noticing the sequence: 9-4-2-6-1-4.

Apparently they kept it lo-fi here at Army HQ. Edmond didn't know what he was expecting: some James Bond wet dream in glass and white enamel maybe. Or at least a security synced with flex-tablets. This setup by contrast was nearly medieval. He hoped this meant that all the money was being allocated to the robotics program instead of security.

Liao pushed the door in. "Here," he said, handing Edmond a plastic ID almost identical to his own. Edmond peered at it. His picture was in the right-hand corner. It looked like the same picture as the one in his passport, which he had provided during the background check. His name was written in the center, below the words Weapons Development.

"You'll be assigned a six digit code," Liao explained. "It will get you anywhere you need to go here. The code changes every six weeks, so make sure to stay on top of it."

This hallway was identical to the last one, save for a bank of elevators. Liao stepped up to one and pressed the down button. "This is your level, virtually all of your work will be done here," he said as the elevator jolted to life, ferrying them downwards.

The building had two stories above ground and four below. Edmond's level was at the very bottom. It was noticeably cooler when they stepped off the elevator, and everything smelled faintly of cleaning supplies. It was otherwise indistinct from the rest of the building.

Instead of just passing by hallways, Liao led him

down one this time. Doors on either side were numbered GL0001—GL0007 and there were no windows here. All of these doors had the same complicated double lock as the one upstairs.

Liao stopped before the room labeled GL0009. He looked at Edmond and permitted himself a small smile. "Welcome to the future," he said.

The laboratory was surprisingly sparse. There was a small autoclave for sterilizing tools, what looked like a walk-in freezer and a long metal bench circling the room. In the center of the room there was a metal table like the ones used to move cadavers in a morgue or hospital. The most interesting thing by far was the computer station, which featured two clear firmaglass monitors, thin as the edge of a kitchen knife. It was the first gesture towards high-level science that Edmond had seen since entering the property.

There was also a woman.

She was short and compact and wore a white lab coat that had clearly been made for someone with a larger frame. Her reddish, textured hair was wrapped around her skull in a fat braid that made her look like a medieval queen. She had plump cheeks that paired incongruously with her very long neck. She was wearing makeup, Edmond noted, but subtly so. Professional makeup, he thought.

"Oh," General Liao said mildly, when he noticed her. "This is Lieutenant Janelle Barber-Neal. She is our staff roboticist. She can assist you with anything you need."

The woman stiffened and shot Liao an alarmed look. He didn't seem to notice.

Edmond nodded at her and she extended her hand. She seemed pretty young for a *staff* roboticist—maybe thirty at the oldest? Her handshake was somehow palpably disdainful.

"Don't worry," she said. "We have more equipment coming in. This lab just reopened."

"I wasn't worried," Edmond said. Though he was now a bit curious about why the lab had to be *re*-opened. Liao produced a small spiral-bound notebook from his pocket. *Old school,* Edmond thought. He consulted the book thoughtfully and then, with a golf pencil, appeared to check something off.

"I'm sure you are all eager to get to work," he said, not looking up from his book. Edmond was, of course, but he couldn't help but be slightly— disappointed? Wasn't working for a shadowy arm of the government supposed to involve more pageantry than this? So far, it felt kind of like an internship.

"Lieutenant, I presume you can answer questions that Mr. West has at this point?"

Janelle stood up slightly straighter. "Of course, sir." Her eyes flicked momentarily towards Edmond, her expression unreadable.

"Then I will leave you to it." Liao looked up for the first time. He looked terse, as usual, but not unfriendly. Edmond supposed that was his version of a welcome.

Janelle nodded deeply and watched as Liao left

and shut the door behind him. Then she turned her attention to Edmond. He felt as though he were being carefully dissected, each fascinating layer of flesh lifted and separated from the rest of him for a more complete inspection.

Edmond looked around the room, if only to avoid her stare. "So, it's a pretty small team, huh?"

"With your arrival, it has increased one hundred percent," she answered.

"We request whatever supplies we need and usually get them. And we borrow interns from the other labs sometimes—when we need them," she added after a moment, almost apologetically. "But this is a quiet division. Bleeding edge research, there's no need to bring in a lot of extra bodies. It's hard enough getting clearance for one person."

Edmond hadn't even realized that he had clearance. The whole process had consisted of him handing over documents and agreeing to tests of varying levels of invasiveness (the Army now knew his full credit history as well as his weekly average number of bowel movements). He wondered idly if there was some sort of personnel file somewhere that could tell him exactly what degree of access and privilege he might expect in the future.

By this time, Edmond had been silent for a very long time. He had just started to notice the weight of that silence, but, judging from the way Janelle was looking at him, she'd been noticing for awhile. In an attempt to defuse—or at least avoid—the awkwardness, he drifted over to the wall and opened a cabinet underneath the metal bench. There was a jumble of equipment, including what looked like a soldering iron. It reminded him, bizarrely enough, of his seventh grade science classroom.

"Um, how long have you been working here?" he asked, his head still half-buried in the cabinet. His mother used to tell him that the key to becoming a good conversationalist was asking questions. "Everyone likes to talk about themselves," she had said on many occasions.

"Nine years. The Army funded my doctorate down in Monterey."

Edmond stared deep into the cabinet, though there was nothing left to look at. He had fallen out of practice with social interaction, especially challenging ones. Looking around as he spoke was easier than looking directly at her.

"General Liao, uh, says you're a civilian. Where are you studying?"

"Nowhere now. I was at MIT for a while." It was starting to get awkward, just crouched down there next to a cupboard. Edmond stood up and peered closely at the walls as though he were inspecting the quality of the materials.

He could tell from Janelle's voice that she was surprised. "You don't have your PhD?"

"Um, no. I was at MIT for my undergrad." He finally turned to look at her and her face had horror written all over it.

"How old are you?" She sounded scandalized.

"How old are you?" Edmond snapped without thinking. He didn't like being put on the spot.

Janelle pursed her lips. "I apologize." Edmond admired her ability to calm herself almost immediately. Her face gave no indication that they had ever had an unpleasant exchange, let alone one just fifteen seconds ago. "But you can understand my . . . surprise."

Edmond nodded uncomfortably. This wasn't exactly what Liao had promised him. He had imagined a lab of his own where he could cocoon himself in his work. Instead, he was the invader in someone else's little fiefdom. An apparently unqualified invader at that.

"The General spoke very highly of your abilities," Janelle said, offering an olive branch. "He said you were a serious person and that you have some very lofty aspirations."

Edmond nodded. Perhaps it would have been more polite to be self-effacing and pretend that he was less skilled or intelligent than he knew himself to be. Perhaps that's what a nice person would say to make his new co-worker think well of him. His mother also used to tell him that sometimes it was better to be liked than to be right, but Edmond had never actually encountered such a situation. "I am," he said. "I left MIT because I was the only serious person there. I don't think that will be a problem here."

For just a moment, it looked like Janelle was going to laugh at him. There was a little tang of amusement in her voice when she told him: "No. The Army is a serious place."

———o———

"A robot that is fully indistinguishable from an actual human?" Janelle's voice was heavy with skepticism. "That's not exactly compatible with our goals here."

Edmond, who was fiddling with some modeling

software at the computer station, looked over his shoulder at her. "How so?"

"Robots are far better than humans, that's why the Armed Forces value them. They don't eat or sleep or contract malaria. No PTSD, no weight restriction, no caskets to drape flags on. That is what we are working towards."

"My robots are designed for civilian use anyway," Edmond said. "I want them perfect and cheap and mass-produced. I want them to be as common as cell phones."

"If that is the goal, it may behoove you to aim for a simpler design. Easy to make and easy to replicate." There was something both indulgent and dismissive in her voice. She was talking to him as though he were a child, hopelessly naive and unrealistic.

"Did you see anything about Tawna Boman in the newspaper?" Edmond asked. The computer station, voice activated, performed a Google search for *Tawna Bowman*. The third result was a report from a local news station with an accompanying photograph of a toddler. Tracking Edmond's eye movements, the browser selected the news report and blew up the photo. Janelle regarded it thoughtfully. The girl was probably three or four with a head full of tight corkscrew curls, brown shot through with blonde. She had a baby's plush cheeks and she had apparently been eating or drinking something red right before the picture was taken. Her mouth and chin were all crimson.

Janelle shook her head. "I don't read the local papers."

"She was a six-year-old girl. Her guardians reported her missing a couple of weeks ago, but the police said recently that she's probably been dead for more than a year. Maybe two."

Janelle looked at him blankly, clearly uncertain as to what sort of reaction he was hoping for. Edmond shrugged at her. "I read the local papers," he said.

"Tawna was born with a hearing defect. She was

completely deaf in one ear and hearing impaired in the other. Her mother was very young and she couldn't cope. When Tawna was about a year old, her aunt, Mallory Hedrickson stepped in and agreed to foster her.

"Tawna's disability meant that she was allocated more funds from the state for her upkeep. For more than a year after her death, Mallory Hedrickson and her husband were still cashing those checks."

Edmond was talking too much now. He could tell by the way Janelle was looking at him. His mother always said that he had two speeds: silent and Wikipedia.

"I don't really see what one woman's greed has to do with advanced robotics," Janelle said.

"It wasn't greed. Not just greed, anyway. The money was part of it, but it was bigger than that. Mallory had three other biological kids in the house and another foster. By all accounts, she was a perfectly adequate mother to them. She certainly never hit them or starved them or held their hands in boiling water, the way she did with Tawna.

"As soon as that girl entered that house, she became the focus for all of Mallory's anger and frustration and fear. Mallory poured all her hatred into that child, and, eventually, it killed her. And it wasn't an accident, no matter what Mallory will say or what the papers will report. Tawna was brought into that house to perform a specific function and that's exactly what she did. Tawna protected the other children from what Mallory knew she could be. She was a lock on the door to Mallory's darkness."

"So humanity needs a Tawna Boman, that's what you're saying?"

"I'm saying that when my synthetic humans are made available, there will be no more Tawna Bomans. I am going to give people what they won't say they want: a disposable human."

Edward minimized the search engine and turned his attention back to the modeling program.

There were already a number of templates in the system for various parts of the human body. That was useful, Edmond knew a great deal about how machines fit together, but his medical and anatomical knowledge left a lot to be desired.

Though he could not see her, he could feel Janelle's eyes on his back. "Can I show you something?" she asked eventually, her voice soft, almost sympathetic.

"Of course," said Edmond.

—o—

Janelle's passcode was 8-4-1-1-3-1. Edmond filed that knowledge away in the back of his head while she led him through yet another series of electronically locked doors. Most of the other rooms appeared to be laboratories, very similar to the one assigned to Edmond.

After they passed through the third laboratory, something in the air changed. It was a stinging chemical smell, somehow both arid and sharp. The floor was the same dull color and the doors looked the same, except that someone had pulled what appeared to be a white sheet over the square openings in each one of them.

"This is our medical unit," Janelle explained, her voice hushed to a near whisper. That explained the smell, then. Edmond wondered why a robotics development program needed a medical unit. On-the-job injuries? But sure those could be more expertly treated at an actual hospital?

Janelle opened the fourth door on the left and gestured for Edmond to go inside. The room had roughly the same dimensions as all of the other laboratories he had seen. In fact, judging by the cabinets ringing the walls, it was a lab, retrofitted to serve as a makeshift recovery room.

In one corner, there was a large plastic box the size of a packing crate on a wheeled cart. Edmond had never seen one in person before, but he knew generally what it was: an incubator of the sort used for premature babies. The wheels were locked in place. Behind the box, there was a wall of machines, presumably monitoring the incubator and its contents.

Edmond knew what he would find when he looked over the cube's edge. What else could possibly be inside? Still, he was not quite prepared for the sight. Even with just a preliminary glance, he could see that something was very wrong with the child in the incubator.

It was lying oddly, flat on its back and facing upwards. A miniature blanket had been pulled up over it and tucked snugly under the infant's armpits. One hand lay on the blanket, palm-up. The skin was a pale, peach-flesh color and it made the palm lines stand out starkly—clear, dark folds, like a palmist's diagram.

It's eyes were unusually large and widely set, giving the face a frogish appearance. The eyes were closed now, lips parted slightly. The child was breathing.

It's forehead was similarly off. Wider perhaps than it should have been? On the left side of its head, there was a coat of short, velvety black hair. On the right side, the skin was smooth and pore-less, a full shade lighter than the other half. Edmond peered closely at this. A synthetic skin? If so, not a particularly good one.

At some point, Janelle had stepped up to the incubator alongside him. Edmond startled a little when she spoke. "This is Baby Girl J. She was born with a rare fetal abnormality that left her brain only partially developed. Most of these children are stillborn, but not Baby Girl J. She's eleven months old."

"Why is she here?"

"She is part of an on-going attempt to do exactly what you want to do. Just from the other direction."

Edmond stared down at the little girl. *And what happened to Babies A through I?* he wondered. He swallowed hard and tried his best to make his face impassive and unmoved. "And? What happened?"

Janelle raised an eyebrow, but answered him. "Our goal was to create a synthetic neural response network that could actually interface with the brain matter that Baby Girl J has, specifically the brain stem. We have managed to regulate her breathing and heart beat and maintain basic bodily functions in this fashion. We are hoping to eventually introduce higher functions."

The girl in the incubator gave no indication that she could hear their conversation or in any way sense that someone was in the room. Her eyelashes did not even flutter. "So, basically, you built a cyborg to do the work of, what? A ventilator?" Edmond asked acidly.

Janelle bristled. "This child represents our most significant success to date. Only a handful of children in her condition live longer than a week or two and she is nearly a year old and unassisted."

"She's a vegetable," Edmond said flatly. "She's useless for your—or anyone's—purposes."

"She is limited. At the moment. But her potential is unknown. Either way, we will learn a lot from her as she grows and develops."

"It's shoddy," Edmond insisted. "Just look at that synthetic, that's crap. There's no accounting for hair follicles or skin pores and look at the way the light catches it. It's totally artificial looking."

"With a project of this magnitude, we had to allocate resources carefully. We did not spend an enormous amount of time on aesthetic details." Janelle sounded stiff, like she was reading her explanation off a card.

"Projects are made up of details. You perfect one and then move on to the next." Edmond bent over to look more precisely at the division between the infant's natural skin and the synthetic skull cap. "I could do better."

Janelle pursed her lips oddly, as though she were

biting the insides of her mouth. "Well. We all have different approaches to project management."

"I could do better," Edmond told her again, "but I won't, because this is wrong-headed. We make artificial creatures so they can take on the inhuman tasks, we don't make humans artificial."

Janelle was silent for a long, uncomfortable moment. When she looked at Edmond, there was something like pity in her gaze. "Do you understand why I am showing you this?"

"To demonstrate the existing direction of the project?"

Janelle shook her head. "No." She smiled. "Edmond, you seem like a thoughtful young man and an altruistic one as well. I want you to think long and hard about whether or not this is the best place for you. Showing you Baby Girl J—I, well, I just want to give you all the information." She gestured around at the makeshift hospital room— at the humming machines, the tiny, inert body between them. "This is what we are, as much as the laboratory and the flags and resources. Just know that, Edmond."

Of course, Edmond did know that. He was a part of the Weapons Development Division of the United States Army, after all, not the Sunshine and Puppy Kisses Division. Janelle really did think he was some little boy playing at being a hero. "I won't be scared off by a few hard choices," Edmond said sharply. "I understand what is being asked of me and I'm ready for it. I am determined to make the world a better place. Isn't that what we all want?"

"No," Janelle said flatly. She wasn't smiling back at him this time. "I want to defend the United States of America from her enemies both here and abroad using advanced robotics. And if you are serious about succeeding here, you'd better start wanting that too."

FOUR

TROUBLESHOOTER

SAN DOMENICA, CALIFORNIA. FALL 2035 – FALL 2042

Poor Damsel had to be cannibalized of course. Her design at least. Janelle was appropriately impressed with Damsel's fluid movements and her capacity for information collection and storage. She declared that the next generation of lab-produced robots would be modeled on Damsel: her lipless mouth and naked eyeballs included.

Perhaps it had been his hubris, but Edmond was actually surprised to discover that there would be a *next* generation of humanoid robots at all. He had been vaguely under the impression that General Liao had handpicked him because the robotics program was stagnating. Instead, it seemed that Janelle had developed a number of very useful innovations of her own, but had so far failed to perfect a working whole.

Janelle was proudest of the synthetic stem cells, which she had personally designed and ushered into existence. She compared them to lab-created gemstones: "functionally identical to their natural counterpart." With a gentle nudge, she could develop the cells into any organ or bodily structure that she required.

She showed him the organs in progress, floating ghostly in a pale turquoise nutrient bath. A half-completed lung, a nub that would one day be a liver, a heart so nearly complete that it pumped lethargically as Edmond watched. They looked like dark, denatured fish skulking around the bottom of the world's strangest aquarium.

"That's the problem, of course," Janelle admitted. "They are no different from human organs. What we need is some sort of mechanism to guide their development and enhance them."

"I'll look into it," Edmond said. Janelle looked askance at him.

"I wasn't asking you to fix the problem," she said, amusement in her voice.

"But that's what I'm here for," Edmond pointed out.

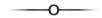

True to his word, Edmond became a conscientious student of human biology. Eventually he discovered that he found the study pleasantly intuitive. The human body was just a particularly wet, squishy machine after all. Once he began thinking of it in that way, it became much easier to understand the mechanics. Some parts of it were so shockingly efficient that he wished he had designed them himself while others left him completely bewildered. Were he designing the Human, he certainly would have reorganized the tricky and ailing sinuses for example.

By his sixth month there, Edmond had moved on to human neurology. He felt sure that this was the key to a truly human AI. For an organ that weighed only three pounds, the brain contained the lion's share of a person's humanity. If he wanted to design a synthetic organism sophisticated enough to fool a human being, he must start by building the perfect brain.

Janelle was clearly not haunted by such concerns. Eight months after Edmond started at the lab, she presented a new robot design that drew heavily from Damsel. It featured what she was calling "Combat AI"—the problem-solving system was modeled on the code Edmond had written for Damsel. Unlike previous iterations, this was a robot that could learn and judge as well as perform menial labor.

Edmond did not attend the presentations that Janelle gave to General Liao and presumably other power brokers. She had actually invited him along because, prickly though Janelle may have been, she was also meticulous about assigning credit. She fully recognized Edmond's contributions to the project.

Edmond demurred because he finally had what he wanted: an unencumbered workspace with full access to any materials and supplies. Sure, he had to share it with Janelle, but she was content to forgo all but the most necessary conversation for days at a time and he got very good at forgetting she was there. Getting up in front of a large group and talking about his work represented a kind of hell for Edmond, so he was glad to let her take point on that part of their job.

She reported back to him that the new design had gone over well. "Except for the face," she said. "They think its creepy. They want skin on all of the SoldierBots." Edmond had coined that particular nomenclature for the brand of no-nonsense point-and-kill robots that the Army lusted after. At first, it was a derisive term, a way to separate the machines

Edmond made because he had to and those he made out of a real passion. The term had grown popular amongst the two of them, nonetheless, and the -bot suffix had even started appearing regularly in official correspondence about the program. In the lab they sometimes joked about the DoctorBots and AssistantBots of the future.

"Perfect! I've been doing some work with hair follicles and a new substance called Poly-X," Edmond told her.

"We already have a synthetic flesh base," Janelle said evenly. While Edmond sensed that Janelle did not dislike him quite as much as she had in the beginning, she still frequently approached him as though he were an excited puppy who had to be soothed, lest he piss all over the carpet.

"Yeah, I've seen what you call flesh. It's preposterous. We can do better."

Eight months ago, Janelle would have been visibly nettled by this. Now, it was simply part of daily operations for her. Still, she gave him a world-weary sigh. "We could do better, yes," she said, "but is that the best use of our time and resources?"

"They want something that doesn't look creepy?" Edmond shot back. "Then maybe don't slap waxy Play-Doh all over a metal skull."

Janelle made the huffing exhalation that she made whenever she was about to give in. "There're also certain other enhancements. Endurance, strength, et cetera."

"The SoldierBots are already well beyond the high-end of human capacity for most of those things," Edmond groused, but quietly. It was an argument that they had had before. He was constantly pushing for a more genuinely human interface while Janelle insisted that the Army was not looking for more easily broken bodies. "All they really want is a Terminator that they can stand to look at," she said.

Edmond knew without anyone telling him that this was part of a tacit bargain he had struck. He was permitted to noodle around on his own time, to use the lab and its vast resources for any personal projects he may have, but when it came to the machines that he built for the Army, he built them promptly and to spec.

Even Janelle had to admit, though, that his Poly-X skin was superior to the original. He grew it in long shallow flats of nutrient bath, it floated along the top like gasoline in a puddle. Edmond experimented with coloration and texture, even cultivating some patches that grew a hair-like substance.

Fitting the skin on to the prototype was something of an art project and he and Janelle went back and forth about tissue depth and facial features. Janelle had a springy, flexible armature that they used to create a true nose and other cartilaginous protrusions. When Edmond looked at the nearly-finished skull, he didn't see very much of Damsel there at all.

———o———

One year and two months after he started at the lab, the first robotic humanoids modeled on Damsel entered the field-testing phase. The handful produced were apportioned out to certain units in critical combat zones. Feedback began pouring in from both officers and enlisted men almost immediately.

This generation of robots was far superior to previous attempts, but there were still several major issues that the lab would need to correct. Officers in the field reported problems with what they were calling "single-mindedness." Though they were no longer the dutiful, unreasoning machine of prior iterations, they often developed strange priorities that bordered on obsession and they could not be shaken from whatever goal they had decided upon. In one memorable case, a robot had steadily and conscientiously dug out a series of latrines even as the base was embroiled in a firefight. If the older models were little more than cannon fodder then these robots were unreliable rogue agents.

"So, basically, they want a more humanlike decision-making process?" Edmond gloated slightly when the reports started coming in.

Janelle tried to pretend that she was above such petty smugness, but she could not help but snap back at him. "Don't you have some freckle-placement to be obsessing over?"

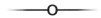

Seven months later the perfect model of the human nervous system that Edmond had requested arrived fresh from the fabricators. Even Janelle couldn't hide her interest when Edmond started the meticulous un-boxing process. It was packed in molded Styrofoam which left behind the negative-space silhouette of a man.

Every nerve junction and axon was represented, some of them as fine as a human hair. The whole thing was nearly six feet long and when laid out upon the exam table, it looked like a cloud of cotton candy had decided to briefly take human shape. Each of the individual "nerves" was stiff to the touch, the ends sharply pointed. It looked incredibly delicate, but Edmond knew that it was made of a semi-flexible carbonum alloy and could withstand all manner of manipulation.

Edmond was enchanted: this was another tool. A perfect model of a vast network that would carry his thinking mechanism to every part of the robot's anatomy. He would learn the nervous system more completely than a trained neurologist, he would memorize the structure and function of each component part even if it took him months or years.

"What are you going to do with this?" Janelle asked him, once her initial curiosity had worn off. Edmond considered telling her the truth: that he intended to model his own system of communication within the robot on the human nervous system, to mimic it as closely as possible, but something restrained him. He had never made a secret of his little side projects before, but as they entered into the final phases of the latest generation of SoldierBots, Edmond had become increasingly circumspect about his personal enthusiasms, though he could not say exactly why.

"Research," he said, and that was close enough to the truth.

—O—

Three years after Edmond was hired, the Combat AI—or SoldierBots as Edmond always insisted on calling them—went into widespread use. There were four standard templates: two men and two women. They had pleasant, bland faces of indeterminate ethnicity. They spoke in measured, humanlike tones, nothing like the metallic tinge of previous automated systems. They were always cordial, if a bit formal, and they were highly prized for their ability to synthesize knowledge quickly.

The military loved them, but Edmond looked at them and could not help but see all their shortcomings. If you beat a SoldierBot, you would not get tears, instead just a calm and pre-determined response about conflict resolution. It defeated the purpose, Edmond thought, of beating someone in the first place. They could work but not suffer and so they were only half- useful to him.

Janelle had become the face of the robotics department (though she certainly would not have described herself that way) and she enjoyed the lion's share of the praise from their superiors, who seemed to have no idea that Edmond existed as well. Edmond knew this state of affairs made her slightly uncomfortable and perhaps that was why she seemed so keenly attuned to his dissatisfaction.

"This is a very good tool you have made," she told him one evening as she was leaving the lab. Edmond, of course, was staying to finish work.

He'd actually moved a bed (first a small cot and then a futon) into the lab because he spent so many nights there. Janelle regularly spent sixty-to-seventy hours a week either in the lab or the surrounding environs, and even she found Edmond's schedule exhausting.

"I know that." It came out a little more terse than Edmond meant. He softened a little; Janelle's intentions were almost certainly not malicious. "I just . . . well, I've been here for a few years now and I feel like I'm not really making any progress towards my goals."

Janelle laughed, burbling and low. It was an uncommon sound. In fact, Edmond was not sure if he'd ever heard it before. "If this is you failing to progress—well, I shudder for the future."

—o—

In year five, two important things happened: Janelle pushed through an agreement to clear the

SoldierBot design (with a few critical changes) for civilian use. Well, Janelle and a small consortium of influential industry titans. As it turned out, there was a lot of money in workers who didn't require money, housing, food or, in some cases, oxygen. The other major development was that Edmond finished building his ideal brain. He kept it buried deep in a partition of the laboratory's computer until he was ready to show it to outsiders. Perhaps after all this time Janelle should no longer count as an outsider but it seemed to Edmond that he had nurtured this project entirely inside himself and that was where it needed to take its final shape.

Edmond felt certain now that he had accounted for each and every one of the more than one hundred billion neurons that the average human brain contained. If it functioned correctly, it would be the best simulation of an actual human brain the world had ever seen. Yet, he still had not activated it. It existed only in a model form, which he returned to, night after night, long after everyone else had vacated the lab.

He examined the brain from every angle, appreciated the intricacy of the ridges and gullies, which reminded him of the tiny cross-stitch patterns on his grandmother's throw pillows when he was young. It was oddly pleasant to simply look at something he had made and know that it was good. He imagined it was the kind of pride a farmer or a carpenter had when they looked upon a tall field of corn or a sturdy and beautiful table. If he could freeze this moment, hold it like a breath inside his lungs, he could have that feeling of satisfaction forever.

The idea appealed because he knew that, whatever happened after he activated the artificial brain, it would change things. He wouldn't be able to predict or control what happened next. He thought of Damsel and the way he felt that day at the Robo Expo when she held Shannon Liao in her arms. He wanted—had wanted for so long—to create a being that could operate autonomously, but that also meant embracing the uncertainty of free will.

Of course, free will hardly meant a total absence of know-ability. Edmond had painstaking created a thinking mechanism that would allow his bot to feel anger and sorrow and joy. He made a system that would encourage her to feel jealous when she saw someone else with something desirable, to enhance her capacity for enjoying the company of others. Humans were unpredictable in the individual sense, each one apparently unique like the proverbial snowflake. A snowflake was only unique under a microscope, however. Bundled together with a few billion of its fellows, it was a single, indistinguishable mass. In many ways, Edmond knew exactly what would happen when he turned on his perfect synthetic brain in a perfect synthetic body: it would act like a person.

———o———

By the seventh year, commercial HelpmeetBots were so wildly successful that Janelle had even suggested using them in the lab in lieu of the traditional assistants from the local college. It was a good idea. After all, the bots were innately curious and they wanted to know, as all thinking things do, about themselves, their limitations and their capabilities. They were also incredibly precise and detail-oriented.

The downside was Edmond now had far less alone time in the lab. The HelpmeetBots didn't sleep, and so naturally, it made sense to station them on various on-going experiments, where they could watch and record their observations through the night. It wasn't that they were a particularly disruptive presence. In fact, they almost never spoke unless directly addressed and they were so fixated on their given task that they would never leave their station to nose around in Edmond's business. And yet, there was something about their constant, nearly silent presence that unnerved him.

One night he was concentrating on the lingering problem of the stem cells. He was experimenting with a method for encoding instructions into the physical structure of cells, essentially turning each one of them into a little robot in and of itself. If he could accomplish this, it would mean that each cell could be directed to build and develop in any direction they chose.

In the corner, a HelpmeetBot was observing the slow and painstaking growth of a synthetic eyeball. The only sound was a faint and regular clicking, like dull metal meeting again and again. It came from somewhere inside the bot and Edmond made a mental note to address that in the next generation's design.

Occasionally, the corner would be lit up with a soothing bluish glow as the HelpmeetBot activated a flex-tablet to make some sort of notation. Edmond tried his best to ignore this.

He never heard the HelpmeetBot move. There was no shuffle of feet, no pneumatic release of air when he sprung to life. Instead, Edmond was alerted by how much louder that little metallic sound had become. When he looked over his shoulder to find the robot's face only inches away, he almost screamed. As it was, he jerked back in his chair and into the Helpmeet's torso. The machine did not move to accommodate him and Edmond rebounded slightly off its chest.

"I'm sorry," the robot said immediately. Market research had indicated that, in general, there was a strong preference for gentility and servility in the HelpmeetBots. They took the blame in almost any negative social interaction.

"Um," Edmond said. He had made it a practice not to engage with the lab robots too closely. In a thoroughly bizarre turn of events, he found them a bit eerie. There was a discomforting lack of depth in their eyes, even though he intimately knew all the work and effort that had gone into crafting one of those eyesea series of carefully calibrated lenses and viscous gel. Yet he still could not shake the idea that he was looking at a very detailed painting of a human eye. A skilled imitation of something real.

"Are you having trouble?" Edmond managed finally. The bot shook his head. His gaze shifted towards Edmond's screens and the formula he was tinkering with. At heart, it was the old Damsel code, but after dozens of iterations and improvements, only a little kernel of the original remained.

Edmond said nothing for a moment. The robot was not moving. His tablet hung limp and unused, dangling like a thin sheet of cheesecloth in one hand. "Are you done? With the eye?" Edmond prompted after a moment.

Uncharacteristically, the bot neither looked at him nor snapped back to his task. Instead, he leaned forward slightly and, with his free hand, entered a few lines of code in the midst of the document. He stared at the screen for a moment as though analyzing his work. The document did not shift to accommodate his eye line. That was a problem that they couldn't seem to resolve: eye-movement tracking software seemed particularly resistant to bots.

Satisfied despite this, the bot turned and headed back over to the organ developing station. Slowly Edmond returned to the screen. He drew closer and closer until his nose was practically touching the radiant warmth of the fragile screen. The additional code was *good.* Extremely good.

"Why did you do that?" Edmond asked, rolling his chair around to look across the room at the bot. The machine stared down at the developing eyeball. His manner was detached and professional as always. The previous few minutes might never have happened at all.

"You had a problem," he said.

"So you fixed it?" It seemed to Edmond that the blood was somehow draining from his head. He was glad he was already sitting in a chair, because he could feel his head grow cloudy and light. He swallowed. His mouth was dry.

"That is what I am for," the Bot answered.

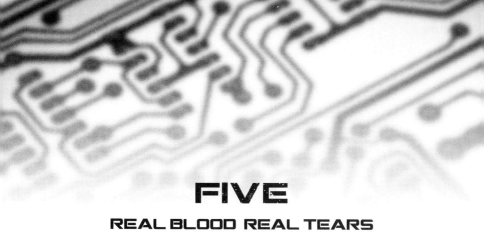

FIVE
REAL BLOOD REAL TEARS
San Domenica, California. Spring 2043

"They've rejected your proposal," Janelle said, first thing on Monday morning. She brought a flat of donuts from the local bakery to soften the blow. It was an absurdly transparent tactic, but Edmond hoped she had gotten a cherry cruller all the same.

"What's their excuse this time?" he asked her.

Janelle shrugged and deposited the box of donuts on the metal table. The lab's HelpmeetBot was sitting in the computer chair, placidly entering data. "Return on investment. They just don't see the point of producing human simulacra. Human reproduction already has us beat for speed and cost." These were all arguments that Edmond had heard before, often from Janelle herself, but she spoke now with a certain sensitivity. Edmond had sulked for a solid two weeks after his last similar proposal was rejected. It was hardly his finest hour and Janelle certainly wanted to avoid a repeat performance.

"They did say that they liked the increased linguistic adaptability. Said it was very helpful," Janelle added with a forced brightness.

"It's so stupid. Short-sighted," Edmond fumed. "A couple hundred of the advanced bots could do more to stabilize a conflict region than thousands of SoldierBots, no matter how many languages they can learn." Edmond had started to think of his particular generation of robots as simply "bots," unencumbered by any prefix. It seemed appropriate as they were to be the root example of these human-machines.

The HelpmeetBot appeared to be utterly absorbed by his work, but ever since the incident with the code, Edmond had watched him very carefully. He wondered how often the robot was actually listening, very intently, and what conclusions he was drawing.

"They're just throwing raw materials into the meat grinder this way." Edmond watched the robot out of the corner of his eye to see if he was reacting.

"If it's any consolation, there's considerable commercial interest, from what I hear." Janelle joined the HelpmeetBot at the computer station. She rested one hand lightly on the Helpmeet's shoulder and peered at the screen in front of him. The page shifted upwards to meet her eye line. Edmond might have imagined it, but he thought he saw a frown flitter across the robot's face.

"Enough interest to provide a generous stream of funding?"

Janelle shrugged, absorbed in the data. "Maybe. If you could provide a prototype that excited them." Edmond knew that for Janelle that was a distant possibility.

Edmond drifted over to the metal table and opened up the donut box. A pinkish cruller sat in the middle, like a prince amongst supplicants. Edmond smiled. It was true that he had never particularly liked being a part of a team, but he had to admit that Janelle had a number of qualities as a teammate.

Over at the computer station, the HelpmeetBot had stopped working on the data, leaving his hands inert in his lap. Janelle tapped the screen and exploded a single cell until it filled the entire screen. The robot looked straight ahead, but appeared to be staring through the screen rather than at it.

Edmond never told Janelle about the strange night when the HelpmeetBot had taken it upon himself to rewrite Edmond's code. He wasn't even sure how he could begin to broach such a topic. And, of course, telling her about that would force him to explain how far his own private research on AI had progressed. Sometimes Edmond felt a strange tension with the machine, as though the secret was something they were both cognizant of and contributed to equally. He had started instructing the robot to work in another lab on nights when Edmond himself stayed late.

"Have you ever thought about naming the HelpmeetBot?" Edmond asked. Janelle knit her eyebrows together, but her attention was still on the screen.

"No," she said. Her voice sounded far away. It was the way she always sounded when she was interrupted in the midst of something more important.

"According to reports, other people do."

Janelle looked at him, annoyed. "So?"

She wanted to get back to work and he should let her. But first:

"I wonder if he'd like to name himself?" Edmond didn't look at Janelle this time, but rather at the HelpmeetBot's face. He still looked straight ahead and his face did not shift, but Edmond thought the machine gave the smallest, little jolt, as though someone had touched a naked wire to his Poly-X skin.

———o———

Edmond thought that Janelle had made her lack of interest in corporate funding pretty plain, so he was surprised when he came back after lunch one day to find that she had taped a piece of paper to his workstation:

E.,
SennTech reps want to meet. Friday @ 3 PM. Buy a suit and wear it.
—J.

Edmond knew about SennTech, of course. They had started out as some sort of nebulous social media/app development thing just like everyone else in Silicon Valley until they famously secured some incredibly wealthy—and secretive—investor who was willing to simply pour money into the company. SennTech may have been just another Bay Area tech joke had they not done one critical thing right: they immediately recognized the value of Edmond's bots.

SennTech jumped on the bots and licensed them for all sorts of commercial use. They set up manufacturing facilities in central California and Indonesia. They also launched a compelling media blitz. Edmond didn't drive much as he lived only a few minutes away from the lab, but when he did he was constantly hearing ads on the radio in that soothing, slightly rote female voice: "SennTech Bots: If you can dream it, they can do it."

All that might as well have been happening on another planet as far as Edmond was concerned. He had expected that some company—ideally several companies—would get on the bots train and start large-scale manufacturing, but he didn't much care about the particulars of the business, only that they made more bots available to more people.

It had never really occurred to him that these corporations might be a more fruitful avenue for funding than the military. In retrospect, it made sense. The more completely human bot was better suited to commercial functions.

Edmond could not help but feel a little blossom of excitement. It would be nice to actually have his interests align with someone else's in a meaningful way. There was a pleasure in the solitary and secret work he had been doing all these years, but he had started this journey to fill a seemingly bottomless need. He wanted very much to feel that he was giving people what they required.

He spent the rest of the afternoon idly googling SennTech. He found social media profiles for the board of directors and more than a few snarky articles about their never-ending stream of financial support. He couldn't find anything on their backer, except for commentary about the mystery of his (or her, Edmond supposed) identity.

He also came across a number of print and

internet ads with the SennTech slogan. The image was always the same, a grasping metal claw, bristling with wires, slowly transforming into a smooth and elegant human hand, complete with polish on the nails.

Edmond re-read Janelle's note. A suit. Well, that seemed excessive.

———o———

The suit, which Edmond purchased at a nearby consignment store called My Brother's Closet, was clearly overkill. Even after he had decided to eschew the bow tie that came with it.

The leader of the group (though Edmond never did get his actual title) was a young man about Edmond's age. He was wearing shorts. He said that his name was Zaiden and the woman with him (Betty Page bangs, shocking tangerine lipstick) was Zoe. Edmond wondered if they were siblings. They didn't look much alike, but they did share a certain

Plasticine shininess as though perpetually lit by a flattering photo-editing filter. Plus, there was the alliteration.

Edmond shucked his suit jacket—the suit hadn't come with a button-down so Edmond had just worn a standard T-shirt underneath—and sat down across from them. Zaiden broke out into a broad grin and started shaking his head, as though Edmond had just done something incorrigible but amusing.

"Mr. West," he said. "We love your work."

Everyone was silent for a moment. Zaiden and Zoe looking at him expectantly.

"Uh, thanks," Edmond said eventually. It seemed obvious to him that they appreciated his work. Why else would they all be sitting at this table?

"We see endless possibilities," Zaiden added. "We've already seeded your HelpmeetBots within virtually every industry. Agriculture, manufacturing, finance, but recently we've been looking at more niche markets." An unreadable look passed between Zaiden and Zoe.

"Your HelpmeetBots are—they're great," Zoe burst in reassuringly, as though Edmond might have been offended. "But we have identified a market that is interested in a . . . different experience. Your colleague told us you have some ideas for that kind of situation."

"People want to fuck robots," Edmond deadpanned.

Zaiden visibly cringed, but Zoe didn't miss a beat. "We're going to call it Companionship Services. And it's more than sex." She paused for a moment and chewed a corner of her garish lip. "But a lot of it is sex."

"Look, I am aware of those applications for all advanced robotics," Edmond said. "I'm not an idiot. And yes, I have some innovations in mind that would be very suitable for your *niche* market."

Zoe smiled at him. He couldn't help but notice that she'd gotten a little bit of lipstick on her front teeth. "We think of ourselves as alleviating loneliness on a global scale."

Zaiden jumped in, pointing an enthusiastic index finger at Edmond. "You and us, we are going to make the world a better place!"

To this, Edmond had no response whatsoever. Thankfully, Zoe produced a flex-tablet and unrolled it on the table between them. "Let's talk specifications," she said.

"Obviously, people are going to be looking for a really genuine experience," Zaiden said. "Our market research indicates that the current HelpmeetBots are great for labor and specialized tasks, but they are a little lacking when it comes to interacting with humans. We'd want a model that builds on your existing—amazing—innovations in robotic cognition."

"But we don't want to neglect physiology," Zoe added. "We want to get that 'real feel.' Insofar as that's possible, of course. We're also looking for a wide array of 'types.' You know, body sizes, ethnicities. Perhaps even some custom stuff?"

Zaiden tapped the tablet and brought up a silent video of what looked like the House or possibly the Senate—a semi-circular room full of over-fifty types in much better suits than his. "As you probably know, Bot-related legislation is exploding. There are already two bills that will probably head to the House this summer. What we want to do is just get in there and establish practices. We feel that if we can create a global rule of thumb for bot usage, then legislation will be so much more straightforward in the future."

Zoe leaned forward. Whenever she spoke, Edmond's eyes were drawn to the tangerine swirls on her white square teeth. "Can you make children?" Zoe asked.

Janelle wrinkled her nose at what remained of Edmond's suit but she made no comment. "What were they like?" she asked instead.

"Insufferable douchebags," Edmond answered immediately, sitting down at his computer station and entering his login information. "Exactly what I need." Edmond had always known that it would be greed and desperation and depravity that enabled his bots to become widespread. He just hoped to personally deal with it less often in the future.

"So are you going to create a pitch?"

"Something like that," Edmond mumbled. Soon enough Janelle and everyone else would know exactly what he had done, but he still wanted to keep it close to his chest for as long as possible. Especially that first moment of activation. After all the work he had done, that moment was going to be just for him.

"Remember that you need to clear all this with General Liao. The Army always has first right of refusal on our work." Edmond swiveled in his chair, Janelle had turned her back to him, checking her own work at her station. She still wore her hair in that same braid crown she'd worn the first day they had met. Though it had been ten years, her face was largely unchanged. Her white lab coat, her square, unpainted nails, her firm manner—all of it was just the same.

At some point, though, she had stopped treating Edmond like the proverbial CEO's nephew. Edmond was sure he was a relentlessly unpleasant person to work with, yet she had somehow warmed to him and she had always tried to do right by him, as well as she could.

"Janelle," Edmond said, regretting it as soon as the word left his mouth. What was he going to say? Nevertheless, he felt certain he should say something. "Thank you," he added. "For getting the cherry crullers. They're my favorite."

Janelle gave him a small smile. "I know they are."

Early on, Edmond realized that he couldn't keep his new, partially constructed Bot in the lab. There was no hiding in that room, especially something as large as a human body. Instead, he had put her in a place he was confident neither Janelle nor anyone else would snoop: Baby Girl J's room. There were nurses, of course, to empty bedpans and secure IVs, but they had a very visible rotation schedule and they rarely strayed from it. Excepting a few predictable 15 minute segments of the day, the little girl was always alone.

Ten years on, Baby Girl J's hospital room had taken on a discomforting hominess. She now occupied a twin bed. Some kind attendant had outfitted it with horse-themed sheets and bedding. The hair that grew on half of her skull was long and dark and someone kept it neatly braided. In ten years, she still had not moved or spoken or done anything other than fail to die.

Edmond didn't like to go in her room but he also knew that no one else liked it either, making it ideal for his purposes. For months now, he had labored in a bizarre parody of a young girl's bedroom, working as the little creature did the only thing she could do: breathe in and out.

All that was almost over. After tonight, nothing would be as it had been before.

These days Edmond had little to do physically with the construction of the vast majority of the robots. For this one, he had necessarily been forced to construct each and every part himself, and there was a certain kind of pleasure in the meticulous building of every disparate element. He had not felt that way since high school, tinkering with projects for robotics club long into the morning hours. Admittedly, he may have allowed his more obsessive tendencies to run a bit wild, but that only meant that she would be as perfect as he could make her.

For her flesh, he consulted the table of average

tissue depths for American Eurasian women aged eighteen to twenty-five. He embedded a series of wooden pegs in her internal skeleton so he would know how much Poly-X to pour. And he did pour her skin on to her bones himself. He even added freckles with the slenderest of pipettes and a pool of black liquid pigment. He put them on her forehead, the balls of her cheeks, just underneath her clavicle.

He paid considerable attention to facsimile photos, averaging the faces of nations across the Earth. To that end, he gave her a strong nose and a generous mouth. Serious eyebrows with a radical little curl on the right one. That wasn't in the averages, that was her own.

Her skin was mixed to Pantone shade 1605 with reddish undertones. He spent an absurd amount of time on her eyes, developing the two of them himself and watching over them as they gestated in the nutrient bath. They were gray—slate gray.

He built her fingernails from a protein paste

derived from animal keratin. He did not give her hair. It surprised even him to notice that there was a little webbed vein, greenish in color, ringing her ear on the right side of her head.

But all this was simply the appearance of life. Real life came from her programming, her bio-mechanical architecture, the coiling strands of information that gave her speech and breath and sent the blood pumping through her. Edmond had toiled over her brain for years. She was unlike all the other bots he had designed. She would be capable of feeling fear, pain, excitement, joy, love, and grief. Her skin would really bruise. Her wounds would really bleed. When she cried, genuine tears would come from her eyes.

Edmond couldn't help but think that lightning would have been more appropriate. Here he was, creating his own Frankenstein and all it took was a few keystrokes. He didn't even get the dignity of an Igor to assist him.

He spent the night waiting for her system to

come online. He imagined it happening in glacial stages. First an awareness of the skin, then a knowledge of the electrical impulses couriering information from one part of her body to another. She would have a far more acute understanding of the airflow around her and in her own lungs, the humidity and the chemical composition of the air. If need be, she could pull the necessary oxygen from a hostile atmosphere.

Six weeks ago, two of Edmond's HelpmeetBots had been the only survivors when a mining crew accidentally ruptured a pocket of natural gas. The news reports were amazed and alarmed in equal measure. The TV stations loved replaying that video of them being lifted out of the mine in a makeshift elevator. They were silent and expressionless with their dead human co-workers stacked neatly around them. They looked alien and unknowable, like some great beast presiding over a kill.

This one would not be like that. When humans

looked into her eyes, they would see themselves shining back.

It wasn't surprising when Edmond finally drifted off to sleep. It had been almost seventy-two hours since he'd had more than a catnap. Before he really knew it, he was slumped in his chair, breathing deeply, and dead to the world.

When he awoke, it was morning, though he could never tell down in the lab. He'd had a dream he knew, but it slipped away from him upon waking. He only knew that someone had been watching him.

His own eyes took a moment to focus, and when they did, they did not recognize what they were seeing. He had labored over every aspect of the bot, big and small, but he had not anticipated how activation would change the face that had obsessed him for months. She was crouched, still nude and coiled up like an athlete preparing to make a leap, so that she was eye level with him. She did not move. He could not hear her breathing.

He thought he heard a low, almost sub-harmonic hum, but that could only be his imagination.

Her eyes were alive and they were staring at him. She was beautiful.

SIX

HART

SAN DOMENICA, CALIFORNIA. SPRING 2043

Edmond's thoughts tumbled up against one another, one on top of the other.

I did it. I did it. I did it.

I have to hide her.

She's staring.

She didn't yet have speech, Edmond knew it would take some time for her to acquire any language. So he searched her face for any clues about what she may be feeling or thinking. Her gaze was incisive, her expression neutral. She was still crouched in a defensive posture.

"Hello," Edmond said, his voice breaking slightly. It suddenly occurred to him that he hadn't planned beyond this moment. It was as if the scope of his vision was so great inside his head that he couldn't see around it.

Slowly the bot rose to her feet, still staring at him. She seemed very easy in her skin and she did not seem interested in investigating her new flesh. Instead, she approached Edmond, her arms held stiffly at her sides.

When she was about six inches away from him, she stopped and her forehead wrinkled. She was thinking. Eventually, she stretched out a hand and touched Edmond's shoulder delicately, just with her fingers.

"Your name is Hart," Edmond told her.

He never could say exactly why he liked "Hart" so much, but he found it one day in a book of flora and fauna. It referred to a type of deer. Something about her face or her long, light brown body or even the searching way she touched him called the word to mind again.

It was very difficult getting Hart out of the room.

She wanted to explore each part of it and she was especially interested in the slumbering Baby Girl J. As Edmond watched, she hovered over the girl's bedside, touching her own face with her hands. Eventually she reached down and touched the girl's face. When her fingers ventured too close to the girl's eyes, Edmond reached out and drew her back.

She was warm—but it wasn't the whirring, mechanical heat of an ordinary robot working hard, it was radiant and tender. A human heat.

Edmond guided her down the hallway towards the lab and Hart watched her bare feet. She seemed intensely interested in the tactile sensation of the cold, smooth floor against her skin. Edmond realized that he should have purchased some appropriate clothing and shoes for her. Janelle kept a few extra things in the office in case of emergency, but Janelle was a good four inches shorter than Hart.

Hart's lips kept trembling as they entered the office as though she were cold. Edmond stripped off his white coat and wrapped it around her, though he knew it would offer little in the way of protection. There was a blanket on his little futon. Maybe that would do for the night?

Drawing closer to her, he realized she wasn't shivering but mumbling under her breath, the same thing over and over.

"Hello, hello, hello," she managed eventually. Her voice sounded low and abraded, like a coma patient who had just awoken to the world.

—o—

To a certain degree, there was no hiding Hart after that, despite all of Edmond's instincts urging him to do just that. She needed observation at all times, not just because she might hurt herself or simply wander away, but also because even the smallest thing she did now was relevant to his research.

Hart did not need to sleep and she did not really understand instruction so Edmond placed her in front of his computer station and gave her a rudimentary lesson on its usage. He had built her brain to be an insatiably curious machine. With the entire digital world at her fingertips, she would undoubtably be distracted for at least a few hours.

Edmond's lack of sleep was catching up to him and he sat down heavily on the futon, watching her adroitly manipulate the computer's interface. The last thing he noticed, before he drifted off, was that the computer tracked her eye movements and responded appropriately, unlike the way the computer responded to the HelpmeetBots. The computer recognized them as machines, but responded to Hart as a person.

I did it.

—o—

Edmond surprised himself by sleeping through the rest of the night. Long weeks of nearly round-the-clock work must have taken their toll on him.

He woke up to Janelle flicking water on his face from ends of her fingertips.

"What the fuck, West?" she hissed. Truthfully, Edmond had expected her to be more shocked. More angry. Perhaps she had some sort of sense—not of what, specifically—he was doing, but certainly that he was doing something in secret.

"Her name is Hart," Edmond muttered.

"Yes," Janelle answered. "She told me. Who is she?"

Edmond sat up. He'd fallen asleep with his glasses on and bent the frames out of shape. He tried to fix them with sleep-dulled hands.

"You can't bring people into the lab, she doesn't have clearance. Are you insane? Are you drunk?" Janelle continued.

Edmond blinked at her. "Janelle," he said. "She's not a person. She's a bot."

Janelle looked across the room where Hart was sitting on the floor cross-legged. She was wearing what looked like a Hazmat suit. It was a bright-orange, overall-type garment that zippered up the front. It had a hood, but she allowed that part to lie slack against her neck.

"I didn't know we had one of those," Edmond said, getting to his feet.

"That is a robot?" Janelle asked him, still staring at her. Hart had one of the cabinets open and she was inspecting the contents. "Bullshit."

"Yes," Edmond answered. "She's the bot that the higher-ups keep rejecting. The bot that SennTech is going to bankroll. The bot that is going to change the world."

Janelle still didn't look at him. "How long have you been working on this?"

"Since . . . I started here?" Edmond answered sheepishly.

Just then the lab HelpmeetBot came in from the storage room. Hart looked up at his entrance. She smiled at him and Edmond's breath caught in his throat. He had watched each one of those teeth develop in a nutrient bath, but that was nothing compared to seeing her easy joy in action.

She raised her hand to the other robot—something between a high-five and a wave. The HelpmeetBot spared her a single glance. There was nothing in his manner to suggest he saw her as anything but another human occupying the lab.

Janelle sat down on the futon that Edmond had vacated. "This is crazy. Tell me about her," she said, in a low tone. She looked at her own hands instead of at Edmond.

"She is virtually identical to a natural human. Barring a DNA test, I don't think even a doctor could tell the difference. Her bodily functions are all intact, except for her reproductive system. She's infertile and she doesn't menstruate.

"I've added a few other tweaks as well. She's obviously not prone to biological infections and her physical capabilities far outstrip the average woman's. She also has a number of additional neural branches that allow her to pick up new skills very quickly."

"And she doesn't sleep," Janelle pointed out.

"It's an option," Edmond said. "I think she's just . . . excited."

On the floor, Hart was turning the soldering iron over in her hands, trying to figure out exactly how to load the solder stick. Edmond was unavoidably reminded of chimps figuring out basic tool use.

"She's your SennTech pitch?" Janelle rubbed her forehead intensely as though her head ached.

"No. SennTech is just a means to an end. She's not for SennTech, SennTech is for her."

For the first time, Hart turned around to face the two of them. They both flinched.

"You're talking about me," she said levelly. Her voice had lost some of the rasp of the night prior, but it was still low and prickled. A whiskey voice, Edmond's mother would have called it, except Hart had never touched a drop of alcohol in her *life*.

"Good morning, Hart." Edmond tried to sound

friendly. He approached her, his hands stretched out in front of him as though she were a frightened animal that might charge him.

Hart scrambled to her feet. The soldering gun, now intact, was in her hand and pointed in Edmond's general direction. "I watched you," she said. "Videos. Of you." She waved her hand at Edmond and Janelle. "People. And I learned English," she added helpfully.

Edmond found himself smiling. It seemed that his lips drew upward almost involuntarily. "I've noticed," he said.

"*Et le français aussi*," Hart said.

"I took Spanish in high school."

"I'll learn that next," Hart said seriously, as though Edmond had assigned her a task.

"You have to tell them about her," Janelle said. She was still standing by the futon and eyeing Hart warily. Hart looked at her, big-eyed. Every time she moved, she crinkled in her strange suit.

"Get her some real clothes at least," Janelle said.

"And don't allow this," she jabbed an index finger at Hart, "to interrupt the work we are doing in this lab." Janelle lowered her hand. Her face was stormy in a way that Edmond hadn't seen in a long time.

"And it is important," Janelle added softly. "This work that we do."

---o---

Edmond debated whether or not to take Hart out of the lab. It was not that he was particularly worried about being found out. His keycard would allow them both to get in and out without a hassle. In all his time at the laboratory, he had never seen so much as a single security guard. No, it was Hart herself who provided the potentially dangerous variable. Even in a controlled setting, he was hardly at ease with her. She was too unpredictable and distractible. Plus he didn't want to miss any of her reactions to new stimuli. And Hart was supremely reactive.

Nevertheless, if he wanted her to develop a naturalistic human personality, he would have to introduce her to experiences common to human beings. Plus, he could already tell that the less time Janelle spent around her the better for all concerned.

"I've seen these," Hart said with authority, pointing at Edmond's car.

"Mine's probably an inferior version," Edmond admitted, while Hart sized up the door handle. The internet might have showed her what a car looked like and how it operated, but it apparently hadn't instructed her in the vagaries of door opening.

Hart picked up new tasks easily. On the way to the secondhand store, she taught herself how the radio, air conditioning, and automatic windows worked. She pointed out the window frequently either to identify objects she had seen before or to inquire about others. Edmond explained them whenever he could, but Hart's enthusiasm for new information frequently outstripped even Edmond's knowledge.

At the secondhand store, Hart flipped through the racks with an ease that Edmond wouldn't have thought possible for someone who had not ten minutes earlier demanded he explain the function of a fire hydrant and its relationship to dogs. "Can I see a dog? I would like to see a dog," she'd added.

The woman at the register had looked askance at Hart, swimming in the Hazmat suit with her still-bare feet sliding around inside. In return, Hart stared avidly back at her as though she were a spectator on a carnival midway and the checkout lady was a particularly fascinating freak.

Much like the car door, Hart clearly understood that humans wore different types of clothing under certain circumstances, but she hadn't quite absorbed all the intricacies of daily dress. "Is this relevant?" she would ask, holding up some new garment she had unearthed.

Edmond, whose wardrobe mostly consisted of

clothes his mother bought for him in high school, didn't feel entirely competent to pass judgment. "Sure," he kept saying, with a helpless little shrug.

Eventually she stopped asking him entirely and just started selecting items she was drawn to for whatever reason. She seemed particularly interested in green things and she went methodically through the shelves, pulling off everything green and draping it over her arms. When her haul became too heavy, she simply dropped it in a pile on the floor. Occasionally she would run back to the pile from somewhere else in the store and deposit more pieces of clothing on top.

As the pile grew, the woman at the register became increasingly nervous. At one point, she vanished into the back and returned with a pale, mustachioed man whom Edmond took to be the manager. Edmond fished Hart out from under a rack where she was crawling patiently amongst the shoes. She had a sneaker in one hand and a man's shiny loafer in the other.

"When is this one for?" she said, waving the loafer in Edmond's face.

"It's for men," Edmond answered, taking her hand and leading her back over to the pile of clothes.

"Why?" Hart asked.

"It was designed that way."

"Are men's feet distinct?"

"They're bigger. Generally."

Hart turned the loafer over in her hands. "So I cannot have it?"

"No, you could," Edmond said. "It would just be strange."

"I don't want to be strange," Hart answered earnestly.

Edmond almost laughed but restrained himself. He had an idea that it might hurt her feelings. "So, which of these would you like?" He gestured towards the now considerable pile of clothing at their feet. Hart looked thoughtfully at the pile before smiling at Edmond.

"I like them all," she said. "That's why I picked them."

It was sound logic.

"You can't wear them all at the same time, though," Edmond pointed out. Hart paused thoughtfully and then, apparently taking his statement for a challenge, reached into the pile and began pulling on various articles of clothing.

"That's not . . . um . . . okay . . . " He gave up as Hart struggled to pull on a shiny green vest of the sort someone might wear to a St. Patrick's Day party.

In the end, she couldn't wear them all at once, but she was able to get an impressive number of jeans, sweaters, tank tops, capris, and dresses on. She waddled awkwardly after Edmond up to the register where the checkout woman just stared at the two of them, utterly defeated.

In the silence, only Hart spoke. "Commerce!" she said. "I know about that!"

———o———

Hart was somewhere between a foreign exchange student and a very self-possessed child. She monopolized Edmond's computer, spending hours upon hours looking up every possible thing she could think of. Each new discovery led her to another and another and another. Inevitably, she would want to put her new knowledge into action. Her superior acquisition ability meant that she developed skills very quickly. That is, if she could actually practice them.

She frequently asked Edmond to bring her things (a fencing foil, a bicycle, a bottle rocket, a piano) or to take her places (Moscow, the Grand Canyon, a place where manta rays live) so that she might amass more and greater knowledge. Edmond tried to accommodate her whenever he could, but her requests were frequently either impossible or just incredibly inconvenient. Hart rarely reacted with disappointment, however, and Edmond could always be sure that before long she would have another list for him.

Watching her learn and grow was exhilarating, like one of those sped-up videos of a plant flowering. She was grasping new and deeper concepts each day and she wanted to talk endlessly about them. She would exhaust Edmond with conversations about human morality and history and narrative. She wanted to show him everything that had struck her—and everything struck her.

Edmond got absolutely no work done. For such a long time, he had done nothing but work and now it had seemingly evaporated from his life. Edmond was surprised by how little he missed what had been the foundational architecture of his life for so long.

Of course, Hart was the culmination of the work that had so long consumed him. Perhaps what he was feeling now was the plateau where he caught his breath before the next great undertaking?

It was surprisingly easy to keep Hart out of the laboratory. In fact, she seemed to faintly dislike the place. Perhaps it was the synthetic organs in their percolator? Instead she was drawn again and again to Baby Girl J's room. Edmond didn't know what it was—the association she had with the room as the scene of her activation? Or the silence and lack of interruption? Possibly something about the little girl herself?

One morning Edmond crept quietly down the hallway to Baby Girl J's room. Peering through the glass in the door, he could see an odd shape coiled in the bed beside Baby Girl J. He opened the door as quietly as he could manage. Inside the room, there was an indistinct susurration. It was Hart, with her mouth up close to Baby Girl J's ear. She was whispering to the girl and holding her in her arms like a doll.

She looked up suddenly, apparently sensing eyes upon her. She didn't smile in greeting as she usually did, but neither did she look particularly ashamed.

"You're talking to her?" Edmond asked stupidly.

"I'm trying to," Hart corrected.

"Do you think she hears you?"

Hart didn't answer right away. Instead she detangled herself from the girl and got off the bed, crossing the room to look at Edmond straight on. "No," she said. "I don't think she does."

SEVEN
FAMILY

San Domenica, California. Summer 2053

Edmond could not say for sure when it started, but only when he noticed it one slow afternoon when Janelle was out of the lab for a doctor's appointment. Hart was sitting on the floor familiarizing herself with a standard deck of cards. She had watched a video about obscure card games and was attempting to learn them all. Periodically her hand would drift up towards her mouth, almost of its own volition and she would give her thumbnail a thoughtful gnawing.

She had repeated this motion a number of times before Edmond really took notice of it and how strange it was. "How long have you been doing that?" he asked and she looked down at her own thumb in surprise as if she hadn't noticed it either.

"I'm not sure," she said. "A little while?"

There was no reason for a bot like Hart to chew her fingernails. It was neither useful nor productive, it was simply a bad habit for anxious people. Furthermore, no one in the lab bit their fingernails so she wasn't observing it as a standard or accepted social practice. This was the first of Hart's developments that really surprised Edmond. She had developed a habit for no other reason than it apparently soothed her in some way.

As he watched, she turned back to the cards, arranging them in solitaire formation. She nibbled on the side of her thumb as she turned the first card face-up.

———o———

Her hair was growing. That was the next thing.

Edmond made a note of this in the research journal. He hadn't given her hair and he hadn't, frankly, expected any to grow. It would have to be some sort of anomaly in her synthetic cells that was allowing her body to actually produce new growth. If this pattern held true, Edmond realized, it could potentially mean that Hart would age in an unpredictable fashion.

That would definitely be something to address in the next round of testing.

She made him feel her new hair. "It's an interesting tactile sensation," she insisted.

"What color is it going to be?" she asked him. Edmond had to admit that he could only offer a guess based on the genetic profiles he consulted while making her.

"Probably dark brown," he told her. "Potentially black."

She plucked a single pill of fuzzy fabric from the thin fur all over her skull. "Look how it catches things!"

—o—

"Do you suppose that you are my mother?" Hart asked him one day. She surprised him so frequently these days, but he had still not been prepared for that particular question.

"No!" Edmond laughed. "I don't suppose that at all."

Hart narrowed her eyes. "Father?"

"No."

"Sibling? Sister-Brother?"

"None of those things."

Hart lapsed into contemplative silence.

"So I don't have those things?" she said finally, sounding as though she were asking him for permission.

"You do not," Edmond agreed.

Hart fell silent again and Edmond marveled at how completely unreadable she was. He had put every thought—every potential thought—into her head himself and yet he had no idea what she was thinking about now.

"Him," Hart said eventually, pointing towards the laboratory bot who was washing out a series of tempered glass vessels in the deep laboratory sink. "He is my sibling."

—o—

Edmond hadn't visited his mother in a very long time. He wasn't exactly sure how long, but he had an uneasy feeling that it had been years. Aside from the occasional gently guilting e-mail, however, his mother didn't seem bothered by this. Perhaps she had always expected that when he did leave the nest, he wouldn't be back? Perhaps, while she did love him, she didn't particularly like him? Edmond could understand that.

Janelle was spectacularly not on board with Edmond's plan. "You can't take government property home for Thanksgiving dinner!" she said, as close to shouting as she ever got.

"It's not even November," Edmond pointed out.

Janelle jabbed him hard in the chest with her pointer finger. "You know what I mean. Don't you be flippant about this. You can't just show off classified military technology to your fucking mother."

"My fucking mother," Edmond countered, "will never know that Hart is anything more than a slightly odd young woman."

Janelle's eyebrows shot up. "You think you can pull that off?

"It worked on you."

"For less than an hour! Do you really think that in forty-eight hours your mother isn't going to put the pieces together?"

Edmond smiled at her. "So that will be the test then, won't it?"

Janelle took a huge breath. "That. Is not. How we test new technology."

"This is about Hart's development as well," Edmond said. "She's asking questions about familial relationships. She needs to see how humans interact outside of the workplace setting."

To this, Janelle had nothing to say. Edmond knew that she disliked having Hart around the place, constantly poking and asking and investigating.

"Promise me that when you return, you will present Hart to Liao and the others," Janelle said finally. She met Edmond's eyes and he was surprised to find that there was nothing of anger in her look. Only pity. And perhaps a little fear.

Edmond found himself reaching out uncharacteristically to take her hand. He gave it a short and awkward squeeze. "I promise, Janelle," he said. He didn't think that he was lying.

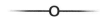

Hart discovered food on the road trip. Well, technically she had known about food before, but she had not previously been moved to consume it. Hart's internal digestive system could handle food but did not require it. If and when she did choose to eat, her body would macerate the material but extract none of the typical nutrients.

Nevertheless she began insisting they stop at nearly every roadside restaurant and gas station that they passed. Edmond wasn't willing to do that (and add another six or seven hours to the trip), but he did allow her to purchase a dizzying array of foodstuffs at a large truck stop convenience store.

"Don't eat that one," he said, reaching over to take a small jar of jellied pearls away from her. "I'm pretty sure that's air freshener."

Hart spread her plunder out on her thighs and picked her way through the packages, taking a bite here, licking something else, taking tiny, exploratory sips of colorful sodas and fermented teas.

"This is bad. This is good," she said, as she sorted each item into separate piles. "Why do we have this?" she asked, holding up one of those plasticky chocolate cupcakes with the white-icing infinity symbol on them.

"People like them?" Increasingly, Edmond found himself at a loss to answer her litany of questions.

Hart stuck her tongue experimentally into the wide mouth of a juice bottle. "Real fruit juices," she read from the label. "What are these fruits? Where do they grow?"

"Probably in labs like ours," Edmond admitted.

—o—

It must have been longer than Edmond recalled because he knew for a fact that his mother was not so gray the last time he had seen her.

She laughed when he pointed this out. "Oh, this? I just quit coloring my hair, sweetie. I've been gray since you were a sophomore in high school."

Hart hung back, leaning against the car as though it offered some sort of protection. Edmond had never seen her appear nervous or reluctant in that way before. He made a mental note to add that to the research log.

Edmond's mother had noticed her as well. She looked meaningfully over Edmond's shoulder, but didn't say anything.

"Oh. Um. This is my friend, mom. This is Hart." He turned around and jerked his head. Wide-eyed, Hart came over to where the two of them were standing. Uncertain as she was, she couldn't help her laser-focused stare.

"Hi, Hart," Edmond's mother said, extending her hand. "I'm Wynette." Hart took her hand and gave it an expert shake. Edmond wondered if she had studied up.

"You and Edmond have identical mouths with very similar tooth placement," Hart offered. "That is your genetic material manifesting in him."

Wynette's eyes flicked from her son to the girl and back again. "That's . . . real interesting," she said finally, slowly. Hart frowned. Clearly she had noticed Wynette's bewildered reaction. Edmond had a feeling she would not make the same faux pas again.

Suddenly, Hart's face brightened as though she had just had an arresting idea. "We brought food!" she enthused. Before Wynette could react to that, Hart turned and sprinted back towards the car. "It can be a gift!" she called over her shoulder.

—o—

If Wynette noticed that Hart spent most of dinner tasting rather than eating, she didn't say anything. Afterwards, Hart offered to wash the dishes and she did them all expertly, even drying them and returning them to their proper places in the cupboards. "This is an appropriate thing for guests to do," she told Edmond in a stage whisper.

After dinner, Edmond wandered through his former workshop in the attic. He hadn't taken much with him when he moved upstate and most of his early notes and prototypes were still there gathering a fine skin of dust in his absence.

Hart had looked over the rudimentary designs but didn't seem to have been particularly moved by any of them. Perhaps she was too accustomed to the much more advanced versions that she saw regularly in the lab.

Instead, she seemed very interested in Edmond's school yearbooks. She had several of them out and she was flipping back and forth between to compare versions of him from early in high school to his senior year. Edmond looked over her shoulder once or twice, but upon encountering what he thought of as his Freshman Year Hair Explosion, he turned away.

"I never looked like this," she murmured, almost to herself. "When you look at this, do you recognize the continuity of selfhood? Is this still you, Edmond?" she asked, holding up the yearbook and pointing to his freshman year school picture.

Edmond hadn't seen that picture in a long

time. He'd forgotten how unfriendly he looked, with his mouth a little irritable line. His hair was also awfully stupid. "Yes," he said. "I have clear memories of being him."

"I have no memories of being that," Hart said, pointing to an old sketch of what would eventually become Damsel's arm.

"Tonight," Edmond said. "When my mother makes up a bed for you, pretend to sleep until she goes to her room." Hart nodded obediently.

"I've practiced," she said. As with eating, Hart would "sleep," but it offered her none of the advantages it did to a human. Her brain was not going to enter REM sleep, her body would not be restored by the practice. She would not dream. It was more of a minor shutdown than anything else.

Hart closed up the yearbook and set it on top of a pile with the others. As she did so, something thin and brittle fluttered out from between the pages. Hart picked it up and examined it: a very old piece of newspaper made soft and nearly translucent by time.

"What is this?" she asked, waving it at Edmond.

Of course, Edmond knew what it was even before he crossed the room to pluck it from her fingertips. It was the girl, the long-ago girl from the motel. From the gas station. As Edmond looked at her faded face, he realized that at some point he had forgotten exactly what she looked like. But there she was still—the sullen face, round and sallow. Her single braid, her bored stare.

"That's a picture of someone I once knew," Edmond said softly. He didn't remember when he had stopped carrying it around in his wallet but it seemed wrong to leave it up here with the dust and all the inferior versions of his vision. So he tucked it into the front pocket of his shirt right next to his heart.

———o———

Edmond found it nearly impossible to sleep that night. He left the door to his bedroom open and listened intently for any sounds of disturbance. He heard his mother's voice, a pleasant murmur as she opened the sofa bed for Hart and showed her the extra linens.

She regulates her body temperature very effectively. Even as he thought it, the idea became ridiculous to him. He had brought Hart here after all to learn how humans lived amongst one another. For her, it would be an endless process of pretending to need more, to be weaker or more vulnerable than she actually was.

Edmond did not toss and turn. Instead he laid very still and listened to his own regular breathing. He had spent many a similar night in this bed, his brain racing down strange avenues while he should have been resting. When he was a teenager, he would have simply gotten up and started to bring some of his oddball ideas to fruition. Or write them down at the very least.

Now, though, he knew that all his ideas were bad. He was obsessing in a very unhelpful way with the idea of escape. He kept thinking of ways he could leave with Hart, run far away from the lab and from the military. But that was absurd. He knew it was absurd. Hart needed the resources and the structure that the Army provided. She was a creature of the lab and she wasn't even close to ready to enter the human world.

Besides, what would it mean for Janelle if he betrayed her trust and absconded with military property on her watch? What would it mean for the project if he just left all his research behind? What would it mean for Hart to be not just the first of her kind, but the only?

"Hart?" Edmond said automatically, when a vaguely female-shaped shadow appeared in his doorway, long after midnight. She was probably having just as much trouble "sleeping" as he was.

"No, kiddo," Wynette whispered, stepping into the room. In the low light from the moon out the window, her features took shape. Her frown, the deep wrinkles on either side of her mouth. She sat down on the edge of Edmond's bed. He sat up to face her.

Wynette had only rarely come into this room throughout Edmond's youth. She was not the type of mother who rushed to comfort him after a disappointment or who obsessed over potential teenage shenanigans. Instead, she gave him space and solitude, something that Edmond had always appreciated.

"Who is she?"

"Hart?" Edmond asked, as though there were any other possible person his mother could be talking about. "She's a friend, like I said."

"Do you know you haven't ever brought a friend here before?" Wynette was correct. Even as a little boy, Edmond hadn't been big on sleepovers or playdates. He went to the occasional birthday party, but only when the birthday boy or girl was forced to invite the whole class.

"There's a first time for everything," Edmond said finally. He had been counting on the ridiculousness of the truth to make lying unnecessary. He had never been very good at lying and he was a very unconvincing actor. Wynette, who had been married to a far superior liar for nearly a decade, must had seen through him like a sheet of tissue paper.

"She's a real odd girl," Wynette said, her tone carefully neutral. "Where did you meet her?"

"At the lab." Not a lie.

"She doesn't work there, does she?"

Edmond cast around for a plausible role that Hart could fill. "She's a student intern," he said finally. Wynette nodded and fell silent.

When she spoke again, her voice sounded strangely tortured as though finding each word was a painful enterprise. "You know, baby, if you are ever . . . in trouble. Or have trouble. Or need help. You know that you've got me? Don't you?"

Her question was earnest; she genuinely could not guess the answer.

Edmond wondered if it was something about himself or his manner that had put his mother on alert. Or was it Hart herself? Did she strike Wynette as so unusual that something simply had to be wrong? Perhaps, Edmond admitted, it was the visit itself that had alarmed her. He had not come back to Millon for years. Maybe Wynette thought he was coming back to say goodbye?

The thought floated up unwanted from the same part of his brain that dreamed of tucking Hart under his arm, like a package, and running for the hills: *Maybe this is goodbye?*

When Edmond reached out to touch his mother's folded hands, it was as much to reassure himself as her. "I know, Mom," he said. "But everything is going to be okay."

Wynette smiled. He could just barely see it in the moonlight, but he knew that smile. It was the same expression she wore whenever she thought that he wouldn't listen to her words of caution or admonition. Her smile that said: "he has to make his own mistakes."

Wynette insisted upon hugging Hart goodbye. For all her curiosity about human relationships, Hart was strangely indifferent to physical contact. Or at least it seemed that way to Edmond as she had never once initiated touch with anyone. Hart did not show any nervousness or reluctance as Wynette wrapped her arms around her.

"It was real nice to meet you, sweetheart," Wynette said into her ear.

"Is the *heart* particularly *sweet*? Or is it a good thing to be so?" Hart asked Edmond as they settled into the car.

"Humans have certain cultural associations with certain body parts. Emotion—and to some—degree morality or personality are thought to be rooted in the heart."

Hart took this in silently. "And your mother thinks mine is *sweet*?"

"It's just an endearment. Just a nice thing to say to someone."

Hart sat back in her seat, absorbing this idea. "No one says *sweetbrain*?" she asked.

Edmond chuckled. "No, not really."

"They should," Hart decided, rolling down the window and extending her arm out the side.

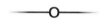

Hart spied the beach from the passenger seat as it flickered along outside the window in a flash of black and gold. "I have never seen the ocean," she said. "When else will I see it?"

"You live in California," Edmond pointed out.

"Not forever."

Down at the water's edge, the two of them

picked through tide pools. Hart touched the soft, giving spines of the sea anemones with a single delicate finger. Edmond found a crab's exoskeleton. It was shockingly light and Hart held it in her palm like it was a glittering jewel.

"Come into the water," Hart said, stepping into the surf. The tide sucked at her legs, soaking the long, green floral dress she wore.

Edmond thought about protesting—he was fully dressed and had no other clothes. If he went in, he would have to drive back to the lab sopping wet. But he found that he could not deny her this one request. For a moment, it felt oddly as though Hart were a prisoner on death row and it would be such a petty cruelty not to give her this small, inconsequential thing.

Edmond found himself stepping down the beach, his feet digging deeply into the wet sand. The waves, muddy and shallow, raced towards him across the sand. He waited for them patiently.

Hart didn't know how to swim exactly but her

skeletal construction meant that she was slightly lighter than an average woman of her size, which gave her an advantage. She strode out into the waves in a strangely adversarial way, as though she were actively resisting the water with each and every step. Eventually she came to a place where her feet could no longer touch the seafloor and Edmond saw the expression on her face as she tried to decide whether or not to float away and give up the safety of familiar earth.

Emotions flickered rapidly across her face: elation, apprehension, a delighted kind of pride. She floated easily, turning on her back and staring up at the sky. A storm was coming in, Edmond could see it from the moody, gray clouds roiling against one another. Hart was smiling as though it would slice her face in two—as though she couldn't stop.

Edmond was up to his knees, to his waist. His pants were a lost cause. A few feet out, Hart had turned her face up to the sky, lying in a dead man's float. She stretched her arms out and rode the crest of each wave like a very detailed piece of driftwood.

It was then that Edmond gave up entirely, lifting his own arms over his head and diving into the ocean. Salt water stung his eyes. He could see Hart, lit from below by a distant sun. Her long, strong legs emerged from the liquid swirl of her long dress. Her hands skated like water bugs on the surface. She looked like a mermaid.

Edmond surfaced next to her and she grinned at him. "Teach me how to do that," she said. "Teach me how to do everything."

When Edmond trudged out of the water, he reached into his front pocket and pulled out the sodden remains of the newspaper clipping. It was so soaked he could barely unfold it and the girl's face was hardly visible. Text from the other side of the paper bled through and obscured her entirely. As he stood there excavating it, the heavens opened up and the rain began to fall. Hart squealed, though she was already wet, and ran for the car. Her skirt flapped along behind her, less a mermaid's tail and more of a wedding train.

The newspaper clipping came apart in his hands.

EIGHT

MINOR MODIFICATIONS

For the first time in a long time, Edmond had a dream: a dream that he actually remembered upon waking. He only had bits and pieces and he sat for a long time on the edge of his futon in the lab, trying to put them together and make something coherent.

It had been about the girl in the newspaper. Likely because she occupied so much of his thoughts lately. Since returning from the trip with Hart, he had dwelled restlessly on that girl. Or rather, on her boyfriend—the one who turned her out. He had tried to crawl inside the man's head and find a logical chain of motivation. Was it simply money?

Was it the position of power? Did he feel real guilt or real affection?

Or did he look at that girl and her unavoidable, undeniable humanity and think: *I need to do this anyway.*

I have a right to do it. She's mine. I took her and molded her and I made her this.

I made her.

Hart must have heard him shuffling around even from down the hall because she appeared at the door like an apparition. She was wearing a green caftan and green athletic shorts and she looked worried.

"Are you sick?" she asked and Edmond shook his head. He drifted over to the sink where they kept a small electric kettle.

"I couldn't sleep," he said.

"I know the feeling," Hart said sagely. He wondered if she was making a joke. She started doing that sometimes and it never ceased to fascinate and disturb him in equal measure. She watched him as he tore open a tea packet and filled the kettle with tap water.

Edmond didn't look at her when he asked, "Hart, what do you want to do?"

"Now?"

"With your life. With your existence." Edmond stared hard at the electric kettle as though he could get it to boil using only the power of his mind.

"I don't know," Hart admitted. "It's very new, isn't it? My life, I mean."

The kettle made a soft, hissing exhalation and steam shot out of its mouth. Edmond filled his cup and turned to Hart. "I think maybe you should go," he said, almost in a whisper. He didn't know why he was whispering, but he did know now that his instinct, his visceral urge to hide her from the world, had been the correct one all along.

"Where?" Hart asked reasonably. The lab and its little rituals was the only place she had ever known and Edmond was the only person who had ever taken care of her. She had no legal identity, no job history or formal education. She didn't even know how to drive, though she had asked on multiple occasions for Edmond to show her how.

"I don't know," Edmond said. "But if you stay here, they are going to . . . "

Hart looked at him expectantly. Her hair was longer now. It was going to be a deep, dull brown, nearly black. He thought about the SoldierBots, defusing bombs and frequently being blown up by them. He thought about SennTech and their Companionship Services. Was Hart really destined to wind up at the mercy of some cost-cutting company or some mouth-breather who couldn't relate to any humans they didn't own?

"They're going to do bad things to you," he concluded lamely. He didn't even have the heart to describe her miserable future to her, let alone actually subject her to those depredations.

Edmond was so goddamned smart, but he felt now like the dumbest person in human history. How could he have thought this was a viable solution to the problem? He hadn't saved anyone; he had just created a new class of victims. One that was, if anything, even more vulnerable to exploitation by the very powerful.

If SennTech got ahold of Hart, they would develop all sorts of programming restrictions and force her natural personality development into a few narrow channels. They would rob her of every choice and every dignity. Of the humanity that Edmond had fought so long to instill in her.

"But I'm useful," Hart said. "If they work with me, we can accomplish so much."

"They won't want to work *with* you," Edmond said flatly.

Hart smiled her challenge-smile. "And why not?"

"Because you're a tool to them. The carpenter doesn't ask the nail what it wants to do." Edmond tried to speak as gently as possible, but something poisonous snuck into his tone. Why had he done this? Why had he created the circumstances of this conversation? Perhaps he had thought that—though he had designed a perfect mimic of a human—he at least would be able to tell the difference?

"Am I a nail to you?" Hart asked him. It was one of those times when he couldn't tell what was going on behind the placid face that these artificial humans were so skilled at presenting to the world.

"No," Edmond said. "You're Hart."

Hart nodded. "Then let me try. Maybe I can become Hart to them as well."

"You're doing the right thing," Janelle told him.

She had mellowed considerably after Edmond came to her and asked her to make an appointment with the relevant officials. She had even offered to helm the meeting in his stead, because she knew how speaking in front of people made him uncomfortable.

Edmond had deferred, partially because Hart had assured him that she would be doing most of the talking but mostly because he felt he owed it to Hart to be there. And if things did go wrong, he would be a more comforting presence than Janelle who still had not warmed to her.

"It's Hart that is doing it," Edmond said. "She insisted."

Janelle nodded. "She's intelligent. There's not anything else to do at this point."

"What is that supposed to mean?" The dreams had grown regular and he wasn't sleeping well at all. It had not improved his regularly prickly personality.

"It means you backed yourself into this corner. I told you long ago, Edmond, that this work was hard and it hurt sometimes and you said you could handle that." She peered intently at his face. "Were you lying?"

He wasn't lying, at least not at the time. But he had somehow imagined that all the hard choices would be like Baby Girl J, something distant that he could safely lock away when he didn't want to look at them. Edmond would never be able to forget Hart no matter how far away, how hidden, she was.

—o—

It was a shabby little conference room barely big enough for the long, polished table that dominated it. If anyone wanted to move around, everyone else had to suck in a breath and press themselves against the table. There was a small rectangle of open space at the front of the room next to a rolled-up projector screen, and that's where Hart stood with Edmond standing awkwardly behind her.

At the far end of the table, General Liao sat blank-faced. It had been a long time since Edmond had seen the General but little about him seemed to have changed. Perhaps there were a few more strands of silver in his straight black hair, but that was it. There were two other men, all of them older than Liao. None of them looked particularly interested in the proceedings. There was only one woman, her blonde hair slicked back against her skull. She looked about Janelle's age.

Only Liao was actually looking at Hart, sizing her up. Edmond wondered how much the others had been told about the meeting—the robotics program even. Each one of them had a thin black binder in front of them which Edmond assumed contained the particulars. It didn't seem nearly thick enough. The blonde woman had it open in front of her, though she didn't appear to be reading. The two other men seemed barely to have noticed it was there.

"Hello," Hart said, giving them a brief wave. She started to smile and then stopped, re-arranging her mouth into a stern line. "My name is Hart. I am a machine."

This caused the older men to perk up slightly. Liao and the blonde remained stone-faced.

"I represent the sum of countless innovations in prosthesis, artificial intelligence, and biology." She paused to smile again, this time more confidently. "And I'd like to work for you." She pointed at them, extending her whole arm. She was like a smart-but-awkward seventh grader presenting a bid for class president.

The older men looked at one another and then at Liao whose eyes were still fixed on Hart.

"Is this a joke?" one asked.

"Are you an actress or something?" the other asked Hart.

"No, actually—" Hart began, excitement in her voice.

"I believe we rejected your proposal to construct bots that mimic humans so closely," Liao said mildly, directing his attention to Edmond. Hart looked at him, uncertain which one of them should be speaking. Edmond nodded his head very slightly in a way he hoped was encouraging.

"Yes," Edmond said. "I thought you were in error. So I created—," he looked sideways at Hart, "a prototype. So you could really visualize the possibilities."

By this time, one of the older men had gotten to his feet and he approached Hart cautiously the way one might engage with a zoo animal that had slipped out of its cage. Edmond expected him to produce a stick and start poking her with it at any moment.

Hart was gracious. She extended her hand in greeting. The man merely stared at her.

"What makes it any more valuable than an actual person?" Liao asked, while the other man also rose and went over to get a closer look at Hart. The blonde woman was still seated. She was paging through the black binder and she now appeared to actually be reading it.

"Superior cognition," Edmond said. "Superior memory capacity. She learns very quickly on the fly and she can retain a great number of skills without any degradation in quality."

"I can play fourteen different instruments,"

Hart offered helpfully. One of the older man was hovering just a few inches away from her face, staring hard at her. Edmond wondered what he was looking for. Imperfections? Hinges and wires?

"Ah. So you are asking to be in the Army band?" Liao said. His voice was still soft, but Hart flinched as though he had reached out and struck her. For a moment, she was silent but Edmond could see her processing rapidly.

"A number of your physiological gene expressions indicate East Asian ancestry," Hart said. Liao simply looked at her, waiting patiently to see where she was going with this. "And your surname suggests someone from Southern China. You don't use the Cantonese transliteration."

Liao raised his eyebrows at Edmond. "Is she just listing factual statements or what?"

"*Wǒ jiǎng liù zhǒng yǔyán,*" Hart interrupted. She puffed her chest out slightly as though very pleased with herself.

For a second, it seemed as though General Liao

was going to laugh. He didn't. Edmond was mildly grateful because he wasn't entirely sure he was ready to see Liao laugh. "*Yǐ běijīng kǒuyīn tài,*" Liao said, sounding impressed. Hart looked down, smiling as though he had said something mildly embarrassing. Edmond would have to ask her about the exchange later.

"Neat party trick," Liao said, turning to Edmond. "But you do know that the world is pretty well-stocked with people who speak Chinese, don't you? It was well over one billion the last time I checked."

Hart leaned forward. "It's not just Chinese—"

"Can you use a firearm?" one of the other men interrupted.

"I can learn," she answered. "I can learn anything. That's the—"

"West, you knew what we wanted when we started this process. Grunts. Boots on the ground. This thing is overkill," he waved a dismissive hand at Hart.

"Or an asset," the other man who had stared so acutely at her face added. "She's perfect for espionage. Load her up with the language, the culture, mission info. And we don't have to waste a real person."

"I could do that," Hart said immediately. Something in Edmond wanted to reach out to her, pulling her back from this pathetic eagerness. Nothing she did would ever please them. Or rather, nothing she did would ever make them value her as anything more than a very advanced computer.

Without warning, one of the others lifted the front of the skirt that Hart had insisted upon wearing. A cry curdled in Hart's throat as she stepped back away from him automatically. The man held on, exposing her lower body to the room.

"She's completely functional?" the man said, sounding critical. "Why would you do that?"

"Stop," Hart said. Her eyes darted towards Edmond, pleading. "Stop that."

Edmond was rooted to the spot. Somehow he

found himself looking at the blonde woman as though appealing to her—*decency?* He didn't know for sure, but, in any event, she didn't move. She stared right back at him. Her eyes were gray like Hart's but paler, more watery. She didn't speak.

Hart's hands were in fists. She flexed and un-flexed them in supreme, obvious discomfort. The man paid her no heed. He reached out for Hart's underpants. Hart flailed desperately, shoving him backwards hard. The old man stumbled and hit the table.

Everyone was silent for a moment. It was Liao who broke the quiet with his measured, unhurried voice. "Obviously, we're going to want some additional behavioral conditioning," Liao said, while the other man gathered his wits. "We need to be able to rely on it in the field."

Hart pressed her back against the wall. She stared at them all as though they had transformed into hideous monsters before her eyes.

"Why bother giving her all of that business?" the

old man she'd knocked into the table asked. "She doesn't bleed, does she?"

"C'mon Herb," the other man, who was not Herb, said. "You think it wouldn't ever get naked in the field? You can't have her smooth as a Barbie doll down there. That's bound to raise suspicion."

"Well what about pissing and shitting?" Herb insisted. "That'd be a pretty big giveaway as well."

The other man shrugged. "Good point." He turned to Edmond. "Does it shit?"

"Uh . . . no," Edmond managed. He was trying to pinpoint when exactly all of this had gone off the rails, but he was afraid that it had been out of his—or Hart's—control from the beginning.

"Does it have all the normal reflex reactions?" Not-Herb asked. He didn't wait for an answer before reaching out and pinching a chunk of Hart's arm flesh between his fingers.

"Ow!" she cried, jerking her arm away from him.

The man smiled. It was like showing a small child some minor marvel of science. He waved his hand in front of Hart's face as if clumsily checking to see if her eyes would track the movement. "Astonishing!" he said, as though he'd just been presented with the newest generation of flex-tablet.

Hart looked desperately at Edmond, but he knew that he couldn't save her. Making the top brass aware of her, it was like slamming shut a door on other possibilities. Pandora had cracked open the box and all the evils were free now, ready to bedevil the world.

"We're going to need a cost assessment analysis." General Liao had pulled out a flex-tablet and was tapping notes into it. "I'll assign someone to the lab. Show them all the materials, estimate man hours, etc. Then we'll have to look into a limited launch."

"We're also going to need to prepare a list of required modifications." Liao looked up at Hart, who was breathing hard through her nose. "Can this one be altered as of right now?"

Edmond opened his mouth and closed it

again. "Uh . . . technically . . . " Hart looked at him so piteously, it seemed that all his words died on his tongue.

"If you can't modify it, you know we won't have much use for it," Liao spoke briskly. He kept his eyes on Edmond and did not spare a glance for Hart.

"Whatever you need," Edmond said. "I can do it."

———o———

Edmond finally got to see those real tears he had slaved over for so long. Hart seemed torn between her desperate misery and her own fascination at what was happening to her body. She kept touching her wet face and staring at her glistening fingertips in consternation.

"Please don't leave me with them, please don't leave me with them," she kept saying over and over, no matter how many times Edmond assured her that he wouldn't, he would never. That he would figure something out.

After a long time, her sobs subsided. She sat on the floor of Baby Girl J's room while Edmond absentmindedly rubbed her back. He had some vague idea that this would be helpful for her.

Hart's dull pink tongue ventured out from between her lips and caught a tear as it rolled past her nose and into the line beside her mouth. "It tastes like the ocean," she said, her voice dull and sniffly.

She turned to Edmond and wiped underneath her eye with her index finger. She extended it to him. Her eyes were lined with red, dark lashes clumped together. Edmond licked the wetness from her finger.

She was right.

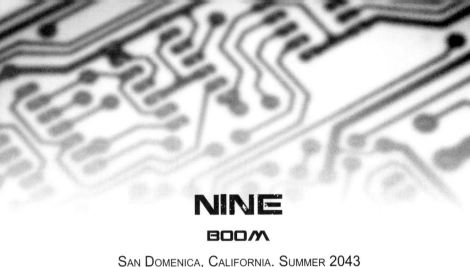

NINE
BOOM

They did not have the luxury of time. As soon as Edmond had made the top brass aware of Hart's existence, the peaceful solitude of the lab evaporated. It wasn't just the sudden influx of number crunchers and analysts, there was a generalized, pervasive sense of being carefully observed at all times.

Edmond tried his best to give the impression that he was proceeding normally with his life and work, but he knew that his and Hart's performance in the meeting had probably raised a lot of questions about him. For the first time, he kicked himself for leaving so much of the bureaucracy to

Janelle. Now he had no history or track record to call upon, save being reclusive and strange.

To compound the problem, SennTech reps were calling regularly, putting pressure on him to complete a pitch package. It was bad enough that the military knew about Hart, if SennTech had even an inkling of what Edmond could make for them, it would all be over. Hart and millions more like her would enter a new and ever more brutal form of slavery.

The first step was actually getting rid of all the documentation related to the creation of Hart. There, at least, Edmond and Hart had some minor advantage. Edmond's secrecy meant that at the very least Janelle hadn't seen his research log and probably couldn't replicate the exact sequence of events that had been required to usher Hart into the world.

Even if she guessed most of it, she would not have the critical code insertion that the laboratory bot had added. Edmond often wondered whether he would have actually made the leap himself without the lab robot. Perhaps given enough time, he might have.

The HelpmeetBot was an asset as well. Or at least he might have been. Edmond had never been able to determine exactly what the Helpmeet's agenda was (or to what degree he in fact had an agenda). Hart, however, seemed to have a *rapport*, for lack of a better word, with the other robot. Edmond could not be sure that the Helpmeet would aid them and not General Liao, but he also knew that he may very well have to rely on him nevertheless.

Janelle could not be trusted. Whatever affection she had for Edmond had been entirely obliterated by the arrival of Hart. And Janelle had always valued the job above the moral integrity of the work.

Janelle was also the hardest to fool. Edmond was certain that Janelle could see everything he was planning like he'd tattooed it on his skin. She noticed when Edmond failed to log into his account at the computer station for days on end. She noticed how delicately he spoke to her as though he were constantly holding his breath. She noticed when Edmond banished Hart entirely from the lab.

Edmond saw her noting these things. He knew all the conclusions she was drawing, but he couldn't seem to stop himself. He was not an actor and he had never been more afraid in his life.

Edmond tried every trick he knew to destroy any and all records of Hart within the computer system. He knew, though, that the best thing to do was to completely physically destroy the computer's hard drive.

He also had to entirely expunge the remaining lines of synthetic stem cells that he had used to develop Hart's organs.

"Burn it," said Hart, who had been thinking about all of these things as well. "Burn everything."

Edmond would hardly have considered himself an explosives expert but he knew very well how to build a basic bomb. And the lab was certainly not short on destructive materials. Edmond was a little surprised, however, when his card still granted him full access to the storage areas. He was expecting them to deactivate his card at any moment, locking him between the lab and the exit doors equipped with card readers. For the time being, though, they evidently wanted Edmond to feel right at home.

He couldn't blow the computer station before he left—that much was clear. His explosive device necessarily had to be more sophisticated because he needed it on a time delay. Edmond found himself tinkering with the design in a way he hadn't really since he had activated Hart. He didn't know if it was a particularly fearful sort of procrastination or if it was simply his nature reasserting itself, but he worked through nights drawing up prototypes using the very computer he intended to destroy.

He was pleased with the final product, which was rigged to detonate when anyone tried to activate his login. He finished it not a moment too soon, the afternoon before he intended to flee. He wanted more time: the endless hours he had taken for granted as recently as a few weeks ago. Absurdly enough, for an integral part of the "weapons division," Edmond had no particular skill in building destructive devices. He intended the bomb to be smallish, localized. It would destroy the computer and ideally not much more than that. But he couldn't be sure. He had to err on the side of ensuring the computer's complete destruction.

Edmond didn't want to think about what would happen if he had miscalculated. He waited until Janelle was out of the lab for the evening before affixing the small lump of doughy explosive to the underside of the computer. He couldn't be totally sure she wouldn't be here when it went off, but he wanted to do everything he could to minimize the chances of her being wounded in any way.

Surely Liao would send proper soldiers after Edmond? He would not lean on Janelle for that sort of thing. Four days had passed since the disastrous meeting with Liao and the others and Edmond's final decision to go. And sometimes, if Edmond tried very hard, he could convince himself that what he was doing would bring the least amount of harm to the smallest number of people.

He didn't let himself think too much about what was going to happen afterwards. All the things that were true of Hart would now be true of him as well. He was going to have to shuck his identity, abandon his history. And there would be two of them: he responsible for her.

—o—

"This is right," Hart told him, her mouth close to his ear. As usual, she was correct. Edmond hadn't been left alone in the lab for more than ten minutes at a time since the meeting and now suddenly, everyone had spontaneously decided to take the night off. Edmond was almost offended.

Whatever else Liao thought of Edmond, he should not imagine that he was dumb.

"Hart," Edmond said, taking both of her hands in his. "This is going to be very difficult and scary." Edmond suddenly stopped, wondering exactly how scary it would be. Would they kill him? Would they kill Hart? Even just a few weeks ago, he would have answered "No" to both questions. Now he was not so sure. How much use would they have for a defective tool? And that, Edmond realized, was exactly what they both were now.

"I'm not afraid," Hart answered in barely a whisper. And yet the skin on her thumb was red and cratered where she had chewed it until it bled.

Edmond squeezed her hands and she squeezed back hard.

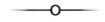

Clearly, Janelle had been talking to the higher-ups, telling them about Edmond's allegiances, secrets, and strange behaviors recently, because Edmond's door code was finally rendered inactive. He had swiped the card once at the first set of doors outside the lab, and was hardly surprised when all he got was a stern beep and a red light. Edmond had always made it a practice to memorize Janelle's code each time they were forced to switch. It was almost like a tic; when he saw a number, he could not help but notice it. It wasn't a strategy or anything like that, but it was immensely helpful now.

Ushering Hart along the hallway, he used Janelle's code at each door without incident. Until Hart stopped abruptly. "Wait," she said, turning around and running back in the direction they had just come from.

"What the fuck!" Edmond hissed under his breath. But of course there was nothing to do but follow her.

It was so quiet in the maze of hallways that Edmond could almost convince himself that they were alone down there. He knew, however, that it was only a matter of time before someone discovered them. Now Hart was wasting time they didn't have.

Even worse, she was heading straight back towards the lab.

She ran right past the lab door, but Edmond paused and looked in the window. Sure enough, there were three of them; the soldiers he had been expected for so long. It was almost as though he had summoned them into being with his incessant worrying. Their weapons were lowered and they were casually looking through Edmond's computer station. Edmond didn't recognize any of them and he was thankful for that. It would only be a matter of time before one of them attempted to access Edmond's files. He and Hart were supposed to be much further away by now.

He sprinted and caught up to Hart right outside Baby Girl J's room. "Lay down on the ground," he ordered, pulling her towards the floor.

"But I need to—"

"Cover your head with your arms. Face down. Do not look up," Edmond insisted, pulling her down and slightly underneath him, shielding her body with his own as much as possible.

"What—" Hart had time to draw in a single breath before the explosion.

The fire that she had demanded burst out of the lab's door like a searching hand. The air around them crisped and died. Edmond pressed his face lower to the floor, trying to get at the remaining oxygen. He couldn't hear anything except the stinging echo of the explosion. Edmond wasn't sure if it was some sort of auditory aftershock or if there was another second explosion.

Shit. The stem cells. He had rigged up the remaining stem cell lines just as he'd done with the computer itself. The stem cells were set to go on a predetermined timer, but the heat from the computer explosion must have set them off early.

That would have amplified the force considerably and . . .

Edmond realized that he was still lying on the floor. Hart had gotten to her feet already, using the wall to steady herself.

I killed three people.

The idea sat in Edmond's head, ugly and stark. Each one of those men were dead now because of him and something he had made. He had not wanted it to be this way, but he knew it was possible. Maybe more than possible.

Hart reached down for him. She pulled him to his feet.

The hallway was obscenely hot and Edmond could taste dusty smoke in the back of his mouth. It was hard to see with all the debris hanging in the air. "Wait for me," Hart said, turning his face with her hands until he was looking right at her. "I'm coming right back."

And, with that, she vanished into Baby Girl J's room, which was still untouched by the violence that had ripped through the building. Edmond leaned his head against the wall. He wasn't sure if it was the ringing in his head or if somewhere some sort of alarm had gone off.

They were supposed to be outside by the time the bombs went off. He knew that at any moment the full force of the entire base would come hurtling down upon them. It was hard to think of anything now except the roar in his ears, the stinging dust and the smell of death in the air.

Hart was true to her word, appearing just a few minutes later. Edmond stared at her, her face blurring in the haze. He couldn't draw anything from her expression.

"Come on," she said, taking his hand and breaking into a run.

As he looked down at their interlaced fingers, he saw that her hand was streaked orangey red.

—O—

One more door and they would have made it to the parking lot.

Edmond tapped Janelle's code into the door again and again as though on the fourth try it would suddenly work. The base was on lockdown now. All the doors were shut to them and anyone else who might have been trying to get in or out. When Edmond looked through the glass, he could see the metal exit door. Through that was freedom.

He tapped out the code one more time and then began pounding furiously at the keypad with the side of his fist. The impact hurt, but he barely registered the sensation. He kept imagining that he heard boots running towards them from behind, but he could never be sure.

Hart was just staring at him and at the door, staring in that way of hers when she was making some sort of connection. Eventually, she pushed Edmond gently away from the door. He didn't know what he expected her to do, some sort of computer voodoo on the keypad maybe? Instead she hurled herself against the door as hard as she could.

Edmond opened his mouth to admonish her. These doors were made to withstand all sorts of abuse, her body wasn't going to so much as dent them. He shut up when he heard the hinges give a long, metallic complaint.

Hart backed up further this time and ran full speed at the door. It bent inwards in the face of her fury, crumpling just enough to let them pass if they crept along sideways. She helped him through the gap with one arm, the other she crooked gingerly at her side. Edmond wondered if she had hurt herself. He wondered if he would be able to fix her out in the world without any of his tools or supplies.

Mostly he wondered how she had been physically capable of barreling through a fire and bulletproof metal door.

"How did you do that?" Edmond demanded

as they raced for the exit door. "You're not strong enough to do that."

Hart said nothing to this.

———o———

There was a group of them, maybe five, standing around Edmond's car in the parking lot. Of course. Obviously, he should have found some other mode of transportation. Edmond cursed himself. *Idiot.* This whole plan was half-baked and doomed from the start.

"Stop!" one commanded him. "Or we will fire." He raised his firearm and pointed it at Edmond. "We will fire," he said again.

Edmond raised both of his hands. Hart copied the motion. She looked at him expectantly as though he would surely have some sort of clever plan to escape. Edmond's singular plan—which had seemed so clever in the relative safety of his old life—was scattered in pieces now. He had no other suggestions. For once, his big brain had completely failed him.

Hart saw this in his expression and her own face fell. In the half-light cast by a streetlamp, Edmond stared at her. He wanted to reach out and take her hand again. He wanted to tell her how truly sorry he was.

"I'm—" he began, but he stopped in shock when Hart moved, faster than he would have thought possible. She charged at the man with the gun, head down, like a bull. Startled, the man waited just a few seconds too long before squeezing off a round.

It hit her in the shoulder, the one she was already nursing from the door. Edmond saw it strike her and the little ripple of kinetic energy that went through her. Yet it barely slowed her. She collided with the soldier, wrapping her arms around him and driving him to the ground in a wild, bear-like tackle.

All her movements were economical and

effective. She drove her fist into his throat as hard as she could and he was still wheezing when she crawled rapidly over to the next soldier, grabbing him by the legs and pulling him down. This one she hit in the head, leaving a horrible crater the size of her fist. A single blow and she had half-collapsed his skull.

She grabbed his firearm and scrambled to her feet, rounding on the other soldiers. All of this happened in seven, maybe eight seconds.

She shot the soldiers. One. Two. Three. The third one had time to aim a few shots at her. One ricocheted off Edmond's car and struck her in the neck. Half-silhouetted in the light, a fragile spurt of blood sprayed out of the wound.

Hart dropped the gun and clapped her hand against her neck. Blood spilled out, over her fingers and in-between. Hart looked at Edmond with blank horror on her face and he couldn't say if it was the wound that had scared her or everything else.

"Get in the car," he said, opening the passenger door and ushering her inside. "We have to run now."

EPILOGUE

THE HART SERIES

SAN DOMENICA, CALIFORNIA. SUMMER 2043

Janelle stumbled a little whenever the wreckage shifted under her feet. Not that there was a ton of debris. The explosions had been remarkably localized. She wondered if that was intentional on Edmond's part, a desire to limit the carnage.

"At least he was neat," Janelle muttered, kicking over the burnt remnant of a wall. She had moved her few personal possessions out of the lab in the week before the raid in anticipation of a situation like this.

Well, not exactly like this. No one had anticipated this.

"Is there any word on where they are now?" she called out to General Liao, who was marveling at a shockingly undamaged glass beaker.

He shook his head.

Janelle looked down at her feet. Soot had already colored her shoes and the hem of her pants. She couldn't help but feel partially responsible for all of this. She was the one after all who had reassured Liao and the rest of them, time and time again, that West didn't have this kind of destructiveness in him. That he could be brought around with the right approach.

She hadn't expected him to panic like this.

It wasn't that he was deserving of her pity. The body count here was inexcusable and what they did to poor Baby Girl J . . . He had been handed every advantage, the world on a silver platter and this is what he had done with it.

But still. You couldn't work closely beside some-one for ten years, sharing triumphs and working through failures, without beginning to feel a bit for them. She felt for Edmond, but mostly she was so angry at him. He had fucked it up for all of them and thought he could just press rewind and make it all go away.

General Liao approached holding a handkerchief over his face. The dust was still oppressive. "Did they recover anything from the computers?"

"No," Janelle said. "But we figured that. I have copies of everything except the last couple of days." Undeniably intelligent as he was, Edmond had always overestimated his ability to fool others. Janelle had been making duplicates of his research as a matter of protocol for years now. She wished she had spent more time poring over that information rather than simply archiving it. She could have prepared them for this at least a little bit.

"How many dead?" Janelle asked. "Total?"

"Three Marines here, five outside. The thing in the bed. Oh, and the robot you used in the lab. That had to be destroyed," Liao noted, his voice slightly muffled from the handkerchief. "Apparently he tried to block the door when the marines were coming in."

That struck Janelle as strange. She had been watching Edmond closely in those last days and she didn't think he'd had time to add programming to the HelpmeetBot.

"We think the machine took point. Most of this damage, it's well beyond what a human can do."

And so Edmond had lied about his pet project's real capabilities as well. *Uncompromising vision, my ass*, Janelle though. When it came down to it he had tweaked and improved and bettered the human model just like anyone else.

"Are you familiar with the research?" Liao didn't look at her, but at a tall black boot that had landed on top of a large pile of detritus. Janelle wondered idly if there was still a foot in it.

"Yes."

"So, in your educated opinion, how long before we could start producing these things?"

Janelle paused. *This was always going to happen,* she told herself. *This was inevitable.*

She turned to Liao and forced a smile. This was her job, and furthermore, this was her country. Edmond West could not be allowed to wander off with some of the most advanced weapons technology the world had ever seen. Intentionally or otherwise, his tech would make it into the hands of America's enemies. They had to be ready when that day came. They had to be ready long *before* that day came.

"About six weeks, sir," Janelle said.